# Bang-Up Season

# BANG-UP SEASON

## A NOVEL

## MARK STEADMAN

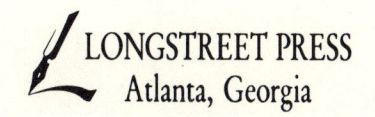

LONGSTREET PRESS
Atlanta, Georgia

Published by
LONGSTREET PRESS, INC.
2150 Newmarket Parkway
Suite 102
Marietta, Georgia 30067

Copyright © 1990 by Mark Steadman

Portions of this material appeared in slightly different form in *A Lion's Share*. Copyright © 1976 by Mark Steadman.

The characters in this story are fictitious, and any similarity to actual people is purely coincidental.

All rights reserved. No part of this book may be reproduced in any form or by any means without the prior written permission of the Publisher, excepting brief quotes used in connection with reviews, written specifically for inclusion in a magazine or newspaper.

Printed in the United States of America

1st printing, 1990

Library of Congress Catalog Number 90-061856

ISBN 0-929264-44-4

This book was printed by R. R. Donnelley and Sons, Harrisonburg, Virginia. The text type was set in Bembo by Typo-Repro, Inc., Atlanta, Georgia. Design by Laura Ellis. Jacket illustration by Walt Floyd.

This book is dedicated to
the many fans of high school football
in the hope that they will buy it.

## AUTHOR'S NOTE

Most of this book appeared in slightly different form in *A Lion's Share*, my second novel, which was published in 1976. Several months after that book appeared, even before the returns began, I had one of those moments of regret that come to writers when it is too late to do anything about them. What I recognized was that the parts of *A Lion's Share* that dealt with the Boniface football team did a certain amount of damage to the overall tone of the work. What I regretted was that I didn't make those parts a separate book.

Now, after fourteen years of thinking about it, I have been given a chance to do that. This time I hope there will be no regrets.

## FOREWORD

Exaggeration, overstatement, hype . . . that seems to be the voice of our times. And it is nowhere easier to see this than in the things that are said about athletic events. There is a game of the year once a week, a game of the decade once a month, and a game of the century once a year — at least. It is necessary for you to understand this in order to appreciate the extraordinary accuracy of the events in the following narration. Here we actually do have a . . .

BANG-UP SEASON!

# 1

Nineteen forty-seven was a pretty good year. Under the Marshall Plan Europe was rebuilding and getting back on its feet. Rationing was over, and the colleges were full of veterans, going to school on the G.I. Bill. Harry Truman was the underdog in the presidential election, but he came from behind to beat Thomas Dewey, thereby confounding the pundits. The New York Yankees beat the Brooklyn Dodgers in the seventh game of the World Series. And, perhaps most important of all, the Boniface College football team had the most riotous season in its history.

Boniface College was the Catholic boys' prep school in Savannah, Georgia. It was run by the Benedictine Fathers. The "Fighting Irish" is what they called themselves, and their colors were green and white. They liked to think of themselves as a little Notre Dame, though their actual record as a football team made that difficult, at least in the closing years of World War II and just after. They had had some very good football teams in the past, as the alumni liked to remind them — especially the Horse Rooney championship team of 1942. But, in the meantime, the lean years had come upon them. Four very lean ones to be exact.

"Fighting *Irish*" had the right ring to it and associations that pleased everybody at Boniface but it held up well only if it wasn't examined too closely—though it was certainly a pervasive state of mind.

A fourth of the student body was Jewish, sent there by parents who were convinced that their sons would get a better education at a school that charged tuition than they would at the public high school, which did not. Most of the other three-fourths of the students were Catholic all right, but half of them were Mediterranean and Teutonic, with names like Debennedetto and Cortez and Schultz. The Irishmen were a sizeable plurality, but not a majority by any means. Only the idea they represented set the tone.

It was an interesting melting pot of a student body, in which almost every ethnic group west of the Danube was represented (there was even one boy who was half Chinese)—except that there weren't any white Anglo-Saxon Protestants. And, of course, there were no Negroes. Also, the student body was all male.

Boniface was a military school. All the boys who went there were called "cadets" and had to wear a blue-gray uniform. Military schools were popular in those days. There was a saying: "In a uniform, you can't tell the rich man's son from the poor man's son." Like most sayings, that one was generally true, but not always. There were times when the uniforms themselves gave things away. Some of the boys from large families wore uniforms, or at least parts of uniforms, that had served five or six or even seven older brothers. The fathers at Boniface were understanding and didn't change the pattern, but even so a pair of pants can be let out and taken up only so many times before it begins to give up the ghost. The mothers wouldn't acknowledge that fact. They would give up on the coats, but not the pants. The pants they felt they were able to do something about. The brass never wore out, and sons took pride in wearing the collar insignia of their fathers, polished with Blitz cloths until nothing was left but the plain brass disk, gleaming in the sun. The brass didn't make up for the pants, but it helped.

The Benedictines were more than understanding; they were diplomatic. The hopelessly seedy-looking younger sons were always placed in the middle squads where they wouldn't be so conspicuous on parades. For the officers and noncoms, there were usually alumni, like J. J. O'Brien, who would chip in and help get them enough pieces of clothing so they wouldn't look too bad walking out in front where people could see them.

It was to Boniface that Jack Lynch came back in the summer of 1947, to play out his last year of high school football. Kathleen Lynch had gone to work to send her son out of town to school, on an obscure but tenaciously held principle that "farther away had to be better." The first year she had sent him to a Catholic military school in Alabama. He was big for his age, and he played quarterback that year. But he was so unhappy at the school that she moved him to St. Francis in New Orleans. He stayed there for two years, where they moved him into the line — the first year to end and the second to center. In the three years he was away from home he almost outgrew his father, who was six feet, five-and-a-half inches tall and weighed more than three hundred pounds. In New Orleans they said that when the dormitory was quiet they could *hear* him growing. It was not an original remark. The same thing was said about Leon Hart, the huge tight end from Notre Dame who won the Heisman Trophy in 1949 — one of the very few lineman ever to do so. Still, whether it was original or not, it certainly applied. All of the Lynches were big men. And the women were big too. Kathleen was only a half-inch short of six feet herself.

When J. J. O'Brien heard about Jack, he made five long-distance telephone calls to New Orleans, which was a lot of long-distance calls in 1947. Then he went around to see the Lynches.

"Six feet, *three* inches, madam?" J. J. O'Brien was inclined to be formal in the way he bespoke himself. "Two hundred and twenty-*five* pounds?" He ran his finger over his moustache, smoothing it down. "Madam, the Fighting Irish need — *need* — your son."

He offered to pay the tuition for Jack at Boniface and to buy all his uniforms. He also promised to have him made a sergeant in the cadet corps — so he could play football there in Savannah, instead of wasting himself out in Louisiana. Kathleen couldn't turn down the offer, and Jack wanted to come home anyway because he was in love with Mary O'Dell, whom he had been able to court only during the summers when he was home from school. Being away from her caused him to droop and pine. As usual, J. J. O'Brien got his way.

Boniface alumni fell into two categories. On the one hand there were the members of the small minority groups — the Jews and the Greeks were the largest of those — and on the other hand there were the Irishmen. The first group was generally more prosperous — most of the boys came from families that had money and could send them on to college, where they would study for the law, or medicine, or dentistry, or business administration. A smaller percentage of the Irishmen went on to college, and a lot of them wound up running liquor stores or working for the fire department — making their peace with the world in concession and compromise. Since Boniface was more or less the end of the line for them, the Irishmen were the ones who kept up their interest in the school, coming out to watch the football practices and following the team to out-of-town games. The other group was more inclined to sever its ties once it got away, going back into the smaller groups from which they had come in the first place. They also formed new allegiances at the colleges they attended.

J. J. O'Brien was one of the most prosperous Irish

alumni of Boniface, if not the most respectable — though he *looked* respectable enough. He had graduated just before World War I and had gone overseas with Black Jack Pershing's AEF, in the 118th Field Artillery, a Savannah outfit. Baseball had been the big game when he was coming along, and he had been catcher for the Boniface Windmills, as they called themselves in those days. He was well known around town since Boniface had beaten Oglethorpe High in 1916 — his last year there — and J. J. had hit the home run that won the game.

He came back from France with a limp, for which he had received the Purple Heart — as well as a chest full of other decorations, including one the French had given him. On the strength of the home run, the limp, and the medals, he borrowed enough money to become the Pabst beer distributor for Savannah — going down to the bank to negotiate the loan in his uniform because that way he could legitimately wear his medals. He also carried a cane.

As the Pabst beer man, J. J. got acquainted with prosperity for the first time in his life. Chatham County never did pay much attention to the Volstead Act, selling beer and wine openly and hard liquor only slightly under cover. The marsh creeks around town in the outlying districts, which had served as off-loading places for slaves a hundred years before, were ideal for rum-running, and Savannah became a center for that activity — with J. J. always in the middle of it, skimming off his share, which grew larger every year. He piled up a very big stake, and after Prohibition was repealed in 1933, he expanded into the wholesale liquor business. He also gradually took over all the betting that went on in the white sections of town.

Like most of the Irish alumni, J. J. took a keen interest in the Boniface football team. But, unlike most of them, he was in a position to put up money to support it—giving presents of cash to the football players from time to time, or hiring them in part-time jobs after school, and helping the poorest ones with their tuition outright, so they could go there instead of to Oglethorpe, the public high school. As a present for the school, he bought a print of the Knute Rockne movie with Pat O'Brien and Ronald Reagan, and gave it to them in the fall of 1945. Every year afterwards it was shown to the whole student body at the first assembly of the year, and once a week to the football team throughout the season.

From 1942 on, J. J. had been getting a very poor return on his investment. In all that time, Boniface hadn't managed a winning season. In 1944—the year that Chicken Garfield had come to Boniface as head coach—they had lost seven games. That had been Coach Garfield's best year.

Chicken was a name that he had lived with for a good many more years than he had actually wanted to, and paring it down was something he had thought about doing for a long time. But his life connected with football was bound up in it, and he was afraid to tamper with it as long as his work was in the coaching line—though his record was such that it probably wouldn't have made much difference one way or the other. The only really good year he'd had was his first one. Not the first one at Boniface—his *very* first one.

Coach Garfield's real name was Critchwood Laverne Garfield, which is a whole mouthful of a name and a very big conception—just fine for special occasions, but a little hard to live with on a day-to-day basis. Even his own family couldn't face up to all of Critchwood Laverne.

His father called him Chick, which he liked—and his mother called him Chicky, which he didn't. She could be thickheaded about some things, and names was one of them. Talking to her didn't do any good because putting that "y" on the end came naturally for her. She called his father Dicky and his sister Becky.

The children in the neighborhood stretched his mother's name for him and called him Chicken. At the time, he regarded it as an improvement.

Through high school and on into college, he didn't think about it very much. But toward the end of his college career—he played guard at Millsaps College in Jackson, Mississippi—the notion began to come to him that a name like Chicken wasn't much of a name for a grown man to go by. Elaine was a big help in making it a matter of concern to him.

He started dating her at the end of his junior year, and she brought it up as a topic of conversation more or less all the time. She took the nickname seriously and thought it was undignified. Her outlook on their relationship was high-minded and ambitious in a wearing kind of way; she was very refined and wanted the best of everything for the both of them — names included. Going around with a man that other people called Chicken — to his face — was more than she felt she ought to have to put up with. So her first project for them was to get rid of the nickname. Elaine was not only obsessive about the matter, she was organized about it as well. First, she went to work on Chicken himself, sending him clippings out of the newspapers with the nickname scratched out and "Critch" written in in pencil. The "i" was dotted with a little circle. She also included comments like "A lovely name" and "More *you* to me." Then she widened her scope and started making complaining telephone calls to the *Clarion-Ledger*, though the boys at the sports desk didn't pay a lot of attention to her when she did it and became pretty abusive and sexual when she kept it up.

There were high expectations at Millsaps that he was going to make the Little All-America team in 1941. None higher than Elaine's, who was counting on that to go a long way toward clearing up their problem with the name. She thought that whoever the people were who picked the Little All-America team, they would not be the sort of people who would put a nickname like Chicken on their official list. But he didn't make the team after all — losing out to a guard from Davidson

College in North Carolina. Elaine thought the name itself was responsible and used it to illustrate her point. But she didn't have time to work on it much because the attack on Pearl Harbor came in December, wiping out her main topic of conversation for a while — though World War II never did really get hold of her interest the way changing the nickname did.

He didn't go into the army. A leg injury kept him out. And he didn't go into the navy, the marines, or the coast guard either. Four times he tried to enlist, but they always turned him down. Just walking across a room, his knee sounded like a whole troop of Spanish dancers. And his feet were flat as a bear's.

When the coast guard said no, he gave up on the war and married Elaine in the summer of 1942. That fall he took a job coaching high school in Eclectic, Alabama. On the team that year there was a fullback named Lenny Pigot. Lenny was six feet tall and weighed two hundred and ten pounds. There weren't many college teams around in those days that could have put enough meat up on the line to stop Lenny, and the other D-division high schools that Eclectic played against didn't even bother to try. Most of them figured that just showing up for the game was pretty daring, and about as much as could reasonably be expected of them. Eclectic averaged eighty points a game, and the closest score of the season was 53-12 against Fred High School of Arno, on a rainy night when Lenny felt like he was catching a cold. The next week there was a snide editorial in the county newspaper with the headline "Coasting."

After the season was over, Chicken and Elaine picked out the best offer, moving to the parochial high school in Mobile, where he had a mediocre season in the fall of 1943. But by then the word about the eighty-point games at Eclectic had drifted over as far as Georgia, and the offer came from Boniface. He went there in the fall of 1944 as head coach where he won the first two games, then lost the last seven.

Since that first season, there had been a lot of talk about *building*, but it had been downhill all the way. The local competition wasn't very high-class itself, and for the last three years Boniface had lost to Oglethorpe — with the margin growing every year. That game was played on Thanksgiving Day in Grayson Stadium, and, for the team that won, it was a good season since, finally, the local frame of reference was the important one.

The potential for a good team was there all right, and no one could fault Chicken on the players that he had chosen to fill the positions. He had all the right talents in the right places, but he was not an inspirational leader, and he could never get them to stop functioning as individuals and work as a team. Maybe he was hoping that Pat O'Brien and Ronald Reagan would do that for him, through the movie. But it didn't work that way.

Still, man for man they had plenty to offer.

# 2

The quarterback was Aaron "Bomber" Stern. Sometimes they called him Bomberstern, but generally they called him Aaron. He wasn't the type for a nickname. Savannah has always been very big on nicknames, and only three of the football players at Boniface answered to the names favored by their parents when they were at home. Mostly they were "Rat," or "Snake," or "Fish," or something even more colorful and descriptive. There were three Rats at Boniface and twelve at Oglethorpe, which had a much bigger enrollment, being coed. In fact, two of the Rats at Oglethorpe were girls.

But Aaron was Aaron, most of the time.

He was a tall, rangy boy, with a calm, intelligent face and a great deal of style. Off the field he was a natty dresser—dark blue pegged pants with a maroon shirt were his preference. He was quiet and collected, and he inspired confidence, being president of the student body and commander of Company A. Everyone more or less looked up to him. On the football field he conducted himself with aplomb and presence of mind, and he undeniably understood what the game was about. He had an arm that seemed to have been made by the Winchester Company and could stand on one ten-yard line and throw a football over the other. He could do that all day long.

But with all that poise, and the great arm too, Aaron had a monumental failing that cancelled out all of his natural strong points. He would absolutely run out of the stadium and climb a light tower before he would let a tackler lay a finger on him. Routinely he would fade back thirty and forty yards to throw his passes, and although the fans loved it, and he certainly had enough arm for the distance, he lost a lot of accuracy when he was going for a receiver more than fifty yards away. Half the time a fifty-yard pass wouldn't do much more than get the ball back to the line of scrimmage. And, besides, those fifty- and sixty-yard bombs spent a lot of time in the air. By the time the ball came down, there would be seven or eight people standing there waiting for it, arguing and shoving each other around.

Both of the ends were good — different but good: Frog Finnechairo at left end and Flasher O'Neil at right.

Flasher was the fastest man on the squad. Everybody in Savannah thought he was the fastest man in the *world*. He had a graceful, pointy-toed stride and could do the hundred in 9.9. When the team ran sprints, Flasher would be down to the other end of the field and coming back before he met the first man of the rest of the squad somewhere around the twenty-yard line. And not only could Flasher get down there in plenty of time, but he had such great style doing it: a series of gazellelike leaps more than a run—floating him along above the field—his chest thrown back, windmilling those long legs in slow motion, with every now and then the tip of a toe just brushing the ground.

He also had the reflexes of a bat. Before Aaron even turned around to throw the ball, Flasher would be off the line and twenty-five yards down the field. Since Aaron's sense of encroachment on his space didn't get abated until he could count a minimum of four five-yard stripes between him and the line of scrimmage, that meant at least a forty-five-yard pass every time.

Aaron tried to whisper the signals so Flasher couldn't tell when the ball was snapped, just to slow him down. But Ducker Hoy, the right tackle, was hard of hearing and also quick off the line, and they got so many off-side penalties doing that he had to stop. Anyway, Flasher didn't need to hear. He had peripheral vision that gave him a 250-degree field and could have seen better only if his eyes had been set on moveable stalks, like a crab's.

But, of course, Flasher had weak points that washed out all the good ones—otherwise his jersey would be up in Canton in the Football Hall of Fame by now.

The first failing was a bad habit. Flasher liked to show off. No matter what the play called for, he would break down the sidelines for twenty-five or thirty yards—it wasn't his fault in a way, it was just that he was out there that far before he could do anything about it.

Then he would cut and begin running from one side of the field to the other, to aggravate the secondary and show them how fast he was. Aaron would be back there yelling at him to turn around so he could see the ball coming, but Flasher would be putting it on, running circles around the defenders, who were trying to keep up with him. Three or four times a game the ball would come in when he wasn't even looking, hitting him on the shoulder pads or the helmet and bouncing off. Those were the times that really got to Coach Garfield, though he didn't think too much of Flasher's habits in general. It was thrilling for the spectators, but Boniface never got many actual yards out of Flasher, in spite of all the mileage he put in scooting around in the secondary.

They said around Boniface that he could actually outrun the football and had to slow down for Aaron's passes to catch up with him. But he liked to run so much that he forgot all about what he was out there *for*, which was catching the ball. He remembered often enough that Coach Garfield had to let him play — though the times the ball bounced off Flasher really made him mad, and he would pull Flasher out of the game, make him sit on the bench, and wouldn't talk to him. But he always sent him back in.

The best field position to take advantage of Flasher's talents was when Boniface was around its own twenty- to twenty-five-yard line. That gave a lot of field ahead of him and about the right amount for Aaron to fade back in without running out of the stadium. Aaron could boom the ball out there and let Flasher run under it somewhere around the twenty-yard line going away. He needed a straight stretch to keep from being distracted. The closer they got to the middle of the field, the more time he had to start fooling around, running back and forth. From the fifty-yard line in, he wasn't much use at all.

Flasher's hands weren't all that good, to tell the truth—even when he saw the ball. And he wasn't much on judging distances either. He was all the time running back on the ball and having it sail off ten feet over his head, or sticking out his hands and having it bounce off his chest. Which was different from the times it bounced off when he wasn't looking. Coach Garfield didn't get so upset about those times since Flasher was at least trying to get hold of the ball—though they certainly didn't thrill him to death either.

Frog Finnechairo was the one with the hands, the one Aaron usually went to any time they got inside the midfield line.

Looking at Frog you would think—well, you would probably think all kinds of things, like you didn't know the circus was in town, and what was a freak doing going to Boniface College. The one thing you would never think would be that here was somebody who played end on a football team. Frog was only five feet, seven or eight inches tall, and his build was very peculiar. Two-thirds of his height was from his waist down, like one of those roly-poly toys with a weight in the bottom that you can't knock down. He was a kind of walking optical illusion because, even if you were taller than he was, you felt like you were looking up at him. He was all leg and butt and foot, with just a tiny little chest and a size-five head on his sloping shoulders. His arms were long, though, with hands that looked like feet on the ends of them.

Getting him suited up in a uniform turned out to be one hell of a problem.

Coach Garfield wrote a series of letters to the company that made the jerseys for the team, but he couldn't make clear to them just what the problem was. So they called in J. J. O'Brien, who put in a long-distance telephone call to the president of the company.

J. J. finally got him to understand that what they needed was a size twenty-nine chest, thirty-six sleeve, green football jersey. But then the president of the company said he was sorry, they didn't have a knitting machine that was up to making a jersey that size. So J. J. asked him why not, and the president said he wouldn't even talk about a thing like that where one of his machines might hear him. Then J. J. got mad and said that was a hell of a way to run a company, and he might just buy them out and show them how it ought to be done. And the president said that would be fine, and if J. J. would mail him a check for fifty-eight million dollars, then he could take over and make all the fucked-up-size football jerseys he wanted to.

"Did you say 'fucked up'?" said J. J.

The president said that's exactly what he'd said.

So J. J. got really mad and called the president of the company a son of a bitch, and the president called him one back, and the operator broke in and told them she'd have to cut them off if they didn't improve their language. Then J. J. told her to kiss his ass, too, and slammed down the receiver.

They solved the problem by ordering three jerseys with Frog's number in the biggest size the company could supply. Then they took them down with Frog's measurements to a tailor on West Broad Street to get them altered.

"Is this for a mascot or something?" the tailor asked after they showed him the measurements.

"No," said Quit Deloney. Quit was the manager of the team and the one they had sent on the errand.

"The only thing that those measurements are going to fit is a baboon," said the tailor. "Are you sure you got them right?" He refused to take the order unless they brought Frog in so he could see what he looked like and measure him himself. So they brought Frog in. But it was dark in the shop, and the man took him out on the sidewalk so he could get a look at him where the light was good.

"I'm sorry," he said when he came back in. "It's just that I got stuck once before on a deal like this. It makes you careful," he said. "A guy came in here once—very well dressed. He had Italian shoes."

"Italian?" said Quit.

"Italians make very good shoes," said the tailor. "I asked him where he got the shoes, and he told me they came from Italy."

"I didn't know that about Italians," said Quit.

"They make very good shoes," said the tailor.

"Did you know that, Frog?" said Quit. "Frog's Italian," he said, talking to the tailor.

Frog had a wad of bubble gum in his mouth, and they had to wait while he blew a bubble before he answered. "No," he said.

"Finnechairo," said Quit. "That's his name. I told you. He's Italian."

"Italians make the best shoes in the world," said the tailor, speaking to Frog.

Frog was blowing another bubble at the time, so he didn't answer.

"Well," said the tailor, "this well-dressed guy came in here and ordered a size thirty-two long dinner jacket . . ."

"Thirty-two *long*?" said Quit.

". . . with three sleeves in it," said the tailor.

"Come *on*."

"I know," said the tailor. "But he was so well dressed. After I saw the shoes I knew he could afford it."

"*Three* sleeves?"

"I should have known better."

"He had three arms?"

"No. I told you. He was very well dressed. He said it was a surprise for a *very special* friend."

"Did you see him?"

"I wanted to," said the tailor, "but I was too embarrassed. I didn't know how to *put* it. I thought it sounded funny." He paused for a minute. "The price was *very* good," he said.

"Where was the extra sleeve?"

"On the side. There were two sleeves on the left side," said the tailor. He didn't look at Quit when he spoke.

"I'd really like to see something like that," said Quit.

"It was a trick," said the tailor.

"It wasn't real?"

"He never came back."

"Just tricking you, eh?"

"A jacket with *one* sleeve, I could have put another sleeve on it."

"Yes," said Quit.

"How are you going to take *off* a sleeve? No way you could do it so it wouldn't show."

Quit looked around the shop. "Look," he said, "we have a game Friday. I'll need to get these back by Thursday."

"A coat . . . it's all of a piece you know. You put it together . . . it's a concept . . . a whole thing." He looked at Quit. "I thought I could trust him, you know . . . because of the shoes."

"Well," said Quit. "Listen, we need to have these back by Thursday. We have a game Friday night."

"Wednesday," said the tailor. "You can have them Wednesday." He turned to Frog. "I hope I didn't hurt your feelings, young man," he said. "I just didn't want to get tricked again."

Frog stopped chewing on the wad of bubble gum and looked at him. "Huh?" he said.

Frog's size-five head gave him a brain-to-weight ratio that was about one leg up on a brontosaurus and went a long way toward explaining a good many of his problems. But, even so, the helmet didn't cause too much trouble. After the hassle they'd had with the jersey, Chicken figured it wasn't worth arguing with the company. So he just ordered the smallest one they made, then pulled up all the inside strapping as tight as it would go, and put in some extra foam rubber for padding and to center it. The way it overhung Frog when he wore it made his head look like a toadstool and didn't help much with the general impression that he made, but it served the purpose. Frog was very happy with it.

The helmet and jerseys made Frog cost three times as much to fit out as anyone else, though the pants and shoes weren't a problem. He wore a thirty waist, with a thirty-five inseam, and size fourteen shoes, which were standard sizes, and only looked peculiar when you saw them on Frog. But they didn't have to explain that to the suppliers, so there wasn't any trouble about them.

What made the investment worthwhile was his hands and his jumping.

Frog was short, but he could outjump Nijinsky. In fact, his height gave him a psychological advantage. He could make a vertical leap of four feet from a standing start. And the really surprising thing was how effortlessly he could do it. One second he would be standing there with his feet flat on the ground, and the next second there would be a swooshing sound and he would be four feet up in the air, stiff as a board, with those number-fourteen shoes of his winged out like he was standing on a platform. With a running start, he could get up in the air five-and-a-half feet.

He wasn't fast, so they used him on spot passes only, sending him out ten or fifteen yards where he would just turn around and stand there waiting for Aaron to get through dodging and faking and throw the ball to him. The defensive back would come over and stand there waiting with him, not able to figure out what was going on because everything was so open and aboveboard. Then Aaron would turn and rifle one to him, putting it about ten feet off the ground, and suddenly the defensive man would be looking at Frog's knees. There would be a splat up there in the air, or the sound of cartilage popping where the ball hit him, and Frog would come down with it wrapped up in that big hand of his.

Frog could usually get the passes with his hands before they got in close enough to do him any damage, but every now and then he would miss. The only time he took one of Aaron's bullets full in the chest all the color drained out of his arms and legs and head and settled in a big blue spot over his breastbone. He walked bent over for a week, coughing up black lumps and talking out of the top of his throat. But it sharpened up his reflexes, so he was always sure to catch the ball with his hands after that, or deflect it so it didn't catch him solid.

Toward the end of the game, there would usually be two or three men out there with Frog, waiting for Aaron to throw him the ball. But when they went up for it, it was always the same story. There would be Frog's pinhead and sloping shoulders up above everybody else, and that thirty-six-inch arm snaked out above that.

Frog's main trouble was that he didn't move too well after he caught the ball, and where he came down is where they usually nailed him. Also his sense of direction left a lot to be desired. He never did know where he was on the field. If Boniface needed twenty-five yards for a first down, Frog would go out and plant himself twenty-*four* yards down the field. He always seemed to be just a long stride short of the first down—though he almost always got the ball. Occasionally somebody would run into him and spin him around and he would go off in the wrong direction. In the game against Bibb High School in Macon, Flasher had to tackle him twice to keep him from running over his own goal line. It was a common occurrence, and Coach Garfield had a "Stop Frog" drill that they used at practice every once in awhile.

On running plays, Aaron's only thought was to get the ball off to the runner as fast as possible, then get the hell out of the way. There was no deception at all to his hand-offs because he *wanted* the charging linemen to see that he didn't have the ball. He would flash it around all over the place before he finally gave it to the back, then he would run off holding both his hands up in the air so nobody would make a mistake and tackle him. Whistler Whitfield and Cowboy McGrath, the left and right halfbacks, complained about it to Aaron and to Coach Garfield. They felt Aaron owed it to them to cover up for them just a little — because the way he waved that ball around on hand-offs they weren't able to make it back to the line of scrimmage more than two or three times a game. Whistler complained more than Cowboy did, which, to some extent, was a matter of temperament since Cowboy was phlegmatic and long suffering by nature. But it also reflected the division of responsibilities in the T formation at that time. The left halfback was the chief ball carrier and general star most of the time while the right half supplied blocking and all-around moral support with much less flash. Whistler felt that the way Aaron behaved was causing him to miss out on the natural share of glory which was his due.

In any event, their complaints never made any impression on Aaron. He was pretty one-track about some things, and he just went right on doing everything he could to make it clear who had the ball — short of calling in a Western Union boy to deliver it for him.

Coach Garfield couldn't do anything with him either, and he worried about Aaron ignoring him that way. But every time he would just about decide to pull him out for insubordination and let somebody else be the quarterback, he would go out to tell him, and there would be Aaron lobbing those sixty- and seventy-yard passes down the field. So he just couldn't make himself go through with it.

The most serious effort Coach Garfield ever made to turn Aaron around was when he got some game films of Frankie Albert running the Stanford T formation. He made Aaron watch them over and over.

"See, Aaron," he'd say. "Who's got the ball?"

"He's *hiding* it," said Aaron. There was pain as well as disbelief in his voice.

"That's right, Aaron," said Coach Garfield. "He's hiding the ball so nobody can tell who's got it."

"That's crazy," said Aaron. "Why would he want to *hide* the ball?"

"That's the T, Aaron. That's what you're supposed to do when you're running the T."

"He played for Stanford."

"What?" said Coach Garfield.

"I never saw Johnny Lujack trying to hide the ball."

Coach Garfield tried to remember whether or not Johnny Lujack hid the ball.

"I guess that's the way they do things out at Stanford," said Aaron. "They wouldn't pull that kind of thing at Notre Dame."

"I want you to pull that kind of thing around here, Aaron," said Coach Garfield. "I really do."

"This isn't Stanford, Coach. Lujack wouldn't pull a trick like that."

While Coach Garfield was trying to remember whether Johnny Lujack tried to hide the ball or not, Aaron got up and left. Whenever Coach Garfield would get onto him about giving the play away, Aaron would look at him and say, "This isn't Stanford, Coach." By the time he got game films of Lujack, the season was over and it was too late to do any good.

As far as Dimmy Camack was concerned, it didn't matter one way or the other whether Aaron hid the ball. Dimmy was the fullback, a Greek boy whose father had a shrimp boat out at Thunderbolt. He was five feet, seven inches tall and weighed 195 pounds. No matter which way you turned him, he seemed to have the same dimensions—frontways, sideways, or upside down. He always ran looking down at the ground, so he couldn't see what Aaron was doing to him anyway. He would rumble by, and Aaron would sock the ball into his gut, dancing off to the side to get out of the way. Dimmy would hit into the line without looking up to see if the hole had opened because, fundamentally, he didn't care whether it did or not. "Hit dat line . . . hit dat line . . ." That was about it as far as Dimmy was concerned. All of the net yards Boniface gained rushing came from Dimmy since Whistler and Cowboy couldn't get out of the backfield, so he was the most valuable back on the team. But more than a few of his teammates thought how nice it would be if they could swap some of Dimmy's heart for just a little more head.

Since Dimmy never looked where he was going, he had to run over whoever happened to be in the way. From tackle to tackle, every Boniface lineman had scars on his back from Dimmy's cleats. The only reason the ends didn't have them too was that Dimmy was too slow to get that far in a lateral direction. He had a gyroscopic sense that told him where the goal was and a kind of mental tunnel vision that sent him straight ahead until enough bodies built up to stop him. He felt that running toward the sideline was almost like cheating — or at least unmanly.

The way he ran, his center of gravity seemed to be down around his knees somewhere, but just the same he inevitably fell on his face on the fifth step, unless he ran into someone — in which case he was good for two or three steps more. There were three yards in it for Boniface every time he carried the ball, but he punished his own team so much they hated to see Aaron give it to him. None of the opposing linemen ever figured him out. They kept trying to tackle him, and all they did was prop him up so he could keep going. If they had just stood aside and watched, they would have cut down on his yardage.

On the nights when Aaron's passing wasn't hitting and he had to call on Dimmy to carry the load, there would be an argument every time they huddled to call a play. Aaron would have to work him back and forth from tackle to tackle to keep his interior linemen from just giving up and walking off the field. Dimmy never knew what they were complaining about. He would stand there in the huddle, flexing his knees and swinging his hands together, saying, "Gimme da ball . . . gimme da ball."

All of the linemen bitched about Dimmy, but none of them complained more than Feeb Siddoney, the left tackle. If the Boniface team was an aggregation of Achilles heels, then Feeb was the heart and core and undiluted essence — totally undipped and exposed — of their collective weakness.

"Feeb" was for feeble, and sometimes for Phoebe, though everybody hated to call a football player Phoebe, no matter how appropriate it was.

Feeb was a big Lebanese, with a nose like a banana and long, black hair that he wore in a ducktail. Not a tall boy, but big, with a strange, humpbacked profile, like a turtle walking on its hind legs. He had large soft eyes, brown like a calf's, and a round baby face. Feeb didn't want to play football in the first place. The only benefit that accrued to him, so far as he could see, was that it let him get into the knickers of a better class of girl than he would otherwise have been able to.

That's in a manner of speaking. Those were pretty innocent times, and the number of girls who were known to put out — actually certified to do it — was extremely small and pretty much limited to the ones who were poor, dumb, and ugly. For them it was an avenue to social distinction — of a kind. They were courted on a more or less one-time basis by young men who wouldn't even look them in the eye or speak to them in a public place. The dates weren't much either — usually a fast run out into the country, where the car was parked under a live oak tree, or in a slash pine thicket, while the line formed at the trunk of the car.

But those were the minority. The great majority were what was known back then as "nice girls." Parking with them down at Fort Screven or on the road to Bonaventure cemetery could sometimes get pretty feverish and slippery but was never much of a threat to the institution of virginity. After he let a nice girl out at her house, the boy would go try to pull up a fireplug, or lift the back end of the car, and if that didn't work, the next night he would get a bunch of his friends together and take the run out to the live oak tree to unload his Fort Screven frustrations.

It could be a vicious innocence, as innocence sometimes tends to be.

Still, as to Feeb, he wasn't all that much of a cocksman. His venality ran more to food than to girls, and he didn't like the frustration of parking at Screven, though he bigmouthed about it as much as anybody else. What he *really* liked to do was sit around Theodore's Ice Cream Parlor, eating chocolate fudge sundaes and talking dirty.

But he weighed 225 pounds — "an eighth of a ton of lard," as somebody put it — and anything that went to

Boniface and weighed that much was going to have to play football, even if it had five legs and a hernia.

His freshman and sophomore years he tried to sneak off into the band and the glee club, but his size made him too conspicuous. He couldn't get away with it. So his junior year, public opinion forced him to pack up his clarinet and go out for the team. There were plenty of 175-pound tackles in those days, and just having Feeb listed on the program gave Boniface a psychological advantage over most of their opponents.

The pressure from the school was fierce, but that was only the half of it. The other half was Feeb's old man, who ran a produce market on Montgomery Street. Somehow when Mr. Siddoney immigrated, he had sloughed off his Levantine guile for a Celtic sense of honor—or maybe it was there, the guile, working itself out in the treatment of his son. At any rate, *he* also insisted that Feeb play football. He put it that the Siddoney honor was involved, though who was going to notice was a good question since there wasn't another Lebanese household within a hundred miles of Savannah. The Siddoneys had visitors from time to time— whole swarthy families that came in a truck with a lot of children in the back. Always they stayed for a week or more, with the children camped out on pallets around the living room and parlor at the Siddoneys', cooking things that smoked up the house and made Feeb's nose run.

"They wouldn't know a fucking football from a fucking eggplant" is the way Feeb put it.

Then he thought about it. "I take that back," he said. "They'd know you couldn't fucking eat the football."

Still, one way or the other Feeb got shoved into being an athlete, and the best he made of it was none too good.

He was useless on defense, except for the times he fell down and somebody tripped over him. On offense he would sometimes be able to get an angle on his man and push him off to the side, but on the plays when Dimmy Camack was carrying the ball, he was more desperate to get out of the way himself than he was to take out his man. There were many times he would come out of the huddle still arguing with Aaron, trying to get him to change the play and send Dimmy off on the other side.

"Hoy, Bomberstern. Let him stomp on Hoy's backbone. Ducker likes it, don't you, Ducker?"

"One man calling signals," said Aaron. "One man calling signals."

"Huh?" said Hoy, lifting his helmet and cupping his hand to his ear.

So Feeb would line up with his head over his shoulder, arguing until the ball was snapped.

For the first two or three plays of a game, Feeb would sometimes bluster and bluff his way, trying to look ferocious and intimidating to the man he was playing against. Saying things like "It's your ass, motherfucker" and "You ain't worth a motherfucking shit." Feeb liked to say *motherfucker*. Maybe it was being Lebanese since they go in very strong for genealogical cursing. But Feeb had a high voice with a quaver in it, and three plays was about the longest he could bring it off. By then the other player would have seen how much of a coward he was and would spend the rest of the night getting even for it. When it was somebody he had played against the year before, Feeb didn't bother with the cursing and bluster but would start dancing around and getting out of the way right off.

As a matter of pure self-interest, Feeb devoted a certain amount of attention to the game. He would study up on the opponents they had to play and would try to get his blocking assignments changed so he could take out the smaller men. He made a disastrous mistake doing that in the season of 1946, when he got Coach Garfield to give him a lot of cross blocking assignments on a little 145-pound guard at Richmond Academy in Augusta. It sounded like a pushover, and Feeb was actually looking forward to the game. But the little man turned out to be pure coiled steel and sharp edges and was so short Feeb couldn't get down low enough either to block him or to protect himself. By the end of the first quarter, he was bleeding out of all eight of his body openings and was backing off the line when the ball was snapped. It got to be so noticeable that even the cheerleaders started commenting on it, and Coach Garfield had to pull him out and keep him on the bench for the rest of the game.

The only game that Feeb looked forward to all year was the one with Glynn Academy in Brunswick, Georgia. That was because the left guard was a 135-pound bantam with weak eyes, and the left tackle, a boy named Delmus Lamott, was even more faint of heart than Feeb himself.

Feeb had nearly gone into cardiac arrest when he saw Lamott's playing weight. "Two twenty-five! Sweet fucking Jesus!" He kept saying "Sweet fucking Jesus" over and over, like it was the password to make a door open to a safe place, but he wasn't getting the pronunciation right. "Sweet *fucking* Jesus . . . *sweet* fucking Jesus . . ." and on and on. Finally, he broke down and cried. Then, when that was over, he tried to think of ways he could weasel out of the game. But no matter how he figured it, there wasn't any way. His father would surely cut him off from his share of the produce business if he disgraced him by quitting the team, and life around Boniface wouldn't be worth living either if he did it. It was one of those terrible, locked-in situations Feeb had devoted his life to avoiding.

He thought about shooting himself in the foot or slamming a door on his finger and breaking it. But of course he was too much of a coward for that kind of thing. So in the end he just skipped practice on Monday and Tuesday, sitting in a back booth at Theodore's, shoveling in one chocolate fudge sundae after another and saying *motherfucker* after each spoonful.

He went back to practice on Wednesday, resolved to get himself hurt bad enough that he would have to miss the game. Not hurt enough to be *really* hurt, but just enough not to have to play.

It was the most furious two days of practice he ever put in in his life. He did everything but run into a wall. The rest of the team couldn't believe it, and Coach Garfield called him into his office to have a talk with him and see what was wrong. He terrorized the B team so much that they all wound up keeping out of his way. The result was that he not only didn't get hurt, but he broke the arm of a sophomore guard. Everybody congratulated him on the way he was hitting, and he told them one and all to kiss his ass.

On Friday night, at Brunswick, he went onto the field crossing himself and praying that he would get hurt early and not too badly, so he wouldn't have to stand up to the punishment for the whole four quarters. When he lined up for the first play of the game, his knees were shaking and the tears were starting in his eyes. The sucking sounds he made trying to breathe could be heard all the way up into the middle of the stands. He knew Lamott was crouched over there across the line from him, but he couldn't bring himself to look up to see.

And then.

Just what he had been praying for all week happened. A miracle. From across the line a dulcet voice, low and whispering and confidential, floated over to him.

"It's only a *game*," said Lamott. The way he said it, it seemed to come out "gwame."

Feeb's heart nearly jumped out of his mouth at sound. Just at the *sound*. He was too frightened to think about the words and didn't hear them at first. Between Monday and Friday noon, when they had left for Brunswick, he had spent a lot of time at the cathedral, burning candles and trying to be holy. But, under the circumstances, he hadn't really put much stock in that. The prayers had all been to get him out of the game. He figured that if they didn't do that for him, they wouldn't help much once it got started.

So he didn't get onto the words that Lamott was saying right away. He looked up into the face of the tackle, which was round and babylike. There was a ghostly pallor to it under the helmet, and big beads of perspiration stood out on his forehead and upper lip.

"What?" said Feeb.

"I hope you remember," said Lamott, his lips trembling, "It's only a game. *I'm* certainly not going to take it seriously."

Feeb looked at him, and he looked at Feeb. Then Lamott's lips twitched and he giggled.

The ball was snapped, and Feeb was so surprised that he forgot to back off the line. Lamott stood up and gave him a gentle shove. "I won't if you won't," he said.

Feeb looked at him, narrowing his eyes. "*Gwame*?" he said. He remembered the week of anguish he had just spent. He pointed his finger at Lamott. "It's your ass," he said. Then he added, "You motherfucker."

On the next play, Feeb was off the line before anybody else, catching Lamott off guard and driving him out of the hole. He danced back to the huddle. "Call it off tackle," he said. "Call the motherfucker off tackle." He slapped his hands together and did a little shuffle.

"What's the matter with you, Feeb?" said Aaron. Ducker Hoy took off his helmet and asked him to say it again.

Dimmy slapped his hands together. "Gimme da ball," he said. "Gimme da ball."

Feeb lined up, making growling noises, looking Lamott in the eye across the line.

"My father is *rich*," said Lamott. He said it in a whisper, but a loud one. He darted his eyes right and left as he spoke.

"What?" said Feeb. "You motherfucker."

"I'll pay you five dollars," Lamott whispered, "not to hurt me."

Feeb looked at him levelly, then he darted his eyes right and left. "Fifteen," he said, also whispering.

They stood there dickering over the price while the ball was snapped. Then Aaron gave Dimmy the ball, and he crashed into Feeb from the back, knocking him down along with Lamott. Lamott helped him up.

"Ten?" he said, holding Feeb's hand and giving him a significant look.

Feeb got his breath back and nodded. "Eleven-fifty," he said.

"Shake on it?" said Lamott.

Feeb nodded again. "Maybe I should get it in writing," he said.

Lamott gave him a playful little shove, then adjusted his helmet. "Football is a *terrible* game," he said.

"What are you doing here then?"

"My father," said Lamott.

"I see," said Feeb. It was something he could relate to.

Lamott's father was indeed rich. He had paid for the uniforms for the whole team and had bought the scoreboard, which had an alligator on it that wagged its tail and lit up with red light bulbs for its eyes and made roaring noises when the Brunswick team scored a touchdown. Under the circumstances, the coach felt that he had to let Delmus play on the team. It didn't work out so badly.

In many respects, Delmus was a chip off the old block, reasoning that if his father could use his money to buy him onto the team, then he could use *his* money to buy himself safety on the field. It cost him about eighty-five dollars a week during the football season, which was a sizable amount at the time. The minimum wage was fifty cents an hour, and the average starting salary for a college graduate was about $225 a month. Still, it was not more than Delmus could afford. He stole most of it from his mother, and he figured it was money well spent. All of the Brunswick players on the first and second teams got paid two dollars a game, more or less so they would keep their mouths shut. He paid the fullback, James Farney, fifteen. James backed up the line on Delmus's side, and it was his job to rush in and take the punishment. Fifteen dollars was an unheard of amount of money for a single night's work that didn't run the risk of either a jail sentence or deportation, but even so James Farney gave good value though he certainly had to shake a leg to do it and wasn't much account at the paper mill on Saturday. Delmus was always dropping hints to James about how he was going to give him a nice soft job there when old man Lamott died and he took over. When Delmus told him that, it made James hustle more than ever, and Delmus would have to get down and roll around on the ground two or three times during the game just to get his uniform dirty.

The players on the other teams that Delmus had to go up against got anywhere from five to twenty dollars, depending on how big they were and the estimate Delmus made as to their capacity for inflicting pain. He had a shrewd eye in that respect. How good they were at dickering up the price was also a factor, but Delmus was a hard man to get the best of. Still, it was always safety first with him, though twenty dollars was his absolute limit.

In the two years of varsity football that he played for Brunswick, he bought every man he ever had to play against but one—a guard at Jesup High School. But the guard weighed only 140 pounds, and he was so stupid the center had to help him get into his three-point stance before he could hike the ball.

After they shook hands on it, Feeb and Delmus made things look good for awhile, pushing and patting each other and shoving each other around. They might have gotten away with it for the whole game, only Delmus couldn't keep his mouth shut. He kept saying things like "It's so *silly*" and "It's just a *dreadful* game." Until Bo Hoerner, Boniface's right guard, caught on to what was going on.

Bo was a phlegmatic German, who took the game seriously—just the way he took everything else. He was always the first one into the room on the nights they showed the Knute Rockne movie, and for ten straight weeks he cried when the Gipper died. At that point in the film, Bo would stand up in the darkened classroom, blocking out the screen, and say, "He was great, man, *great*." Sometimes in the huddle he would say, "Let's win this one for the Gipper." The team found it depressing because whenever he said it they were at least three touchdowns behind. It never did any good. Still, Bo kept thinking that it might.

The other guard, Chippy Depeau, was too far away to hear the conversation that Feeb and Delmus were carrying on, but he probably wouldn't have said anything if he had. He was the direct opposite of Bo—the quietest and least noticed lineman on the team, which was actually a tribute to him—the way he played. He was the pulling guard—"the fifth man in the backfield" they sometimes called it—and he never chattered or mouthed off during games, no matter how much the other team tried to bring it out in him. In his case, silence was a weapon, and forty-eight minutes of lining up opposite him was a nerve-wracking experience. Compared to Chippy, the meaning of life was an open book; his silence probed the limits of what flesh and blood could bear. In Chippy's presence, the Sphinx would have ended up talking to itself.

Of course, he noticed what was going on between Feeb and Delmus Lamott, but, true to his nature, he never uttered a word. Bo, on the other hand, took a serious and morally oriented view of the matter, and when he finally couldn't stand it any longer, he broke his stance before the ball was snapped to kick Feeb on the rear end. "Listen, Siddoney," he said. "Remember the Gipper."

"Watch out, young man," said Delmus, coming to Feeb's defense. "Keep your hands to yourself." Somehow he got a lisp into *yourself.*

Boniface got a five-yard penalty for it, and Garfield called Bo over to the sideline to find out what had prompted him to behave the way he had. Hoerner cried for awhile at the shame and infamy of it, then he told

Garfield what was going on out there between Feeb and Delmus, and Garfield pulled Feeb out and sent in his substitute, Tally Dehoy, a 140-pound Spanish boy whose father ran a fish market on the east end of Bay Street. Dehoy did a pretty good job of pushing Delmus around until they settled on seven-fifty and a bottle of rosé wine. There were only three quarters left in the game, and Delmus was too much of a businessman to go as high as he had with Feeb.

In the third quarter, Dimmy stepped on Dehoy's hand and broke it, so Coach Garfield had to send Feeb back in. Feeb and Delmus spent the fourth quarter haggling over how much Delmus ought to deduct for the two quarters Feeb had been out of the game, but they did it quietly and with discretion, so Hoerner wouldn't hear and blow the whistle on them again.

They settled on five dollars and twenty-five cents.

Sorry as he was, Feeb was necessary to them in a way. He was the focus and excuse for the collective inadequacies of the team. With him, they had a reason for losing, so they didn't need to feel bad about it. Nor did they need to worry about the burden of winning. No one on the team was up to that—especially Coach Garfield himself. If they hadn't had a Feeb Siddoney, they would have been forced to invent one.

Well, one man on the team was up to winning, but he never got to play. That was Lulu Demarco, the first-string center.

Lulu was the first-string center, but he never got to play because he always got hurt in the first game of the season. He was the best man on the team for spirit—even better than Bo Hoerner because there was a hard edge to him. He was also mean as a snake and a boy who positively lived and breathed for the game of football. The trouble was he was too little to be that mean and get away with it on a football field—or anywhere else, for that matter. He weighed only 135 pounds when his general outlook and disposition called for a quarter of a ton at least.

His outlook came from the fact that Lulu had gotten his growth early, at just the time when he was beginning to decide where he fit into the scheme of things.

When he was thirteen years old, Lulu was five feet, nine inches tall and weighed 141 pounds—which made him one of the biggest boys in the freshman class. Out of that one year's growth developed the way that he looked at the world. But, then, that was the end of it. He never grew any more. Not an inch. Nor a pound. By the time he became a senior, all of his classmates had grown on past him and made him a runt, but somehow he never noticed what had happened. So he carried his big man's perspective along with him, and none of the head-on collisions he had with reality because of it were ever able to knock it out of him.

Two years he started at center, and both years he got carried off the field in the first quarter with injuries that benched him for the rest of the season. In 1945, after eight-and-a-half minutes of the first quarter, he threw a block on a guard that fractured six ribs and broke his collarbone. In 1946, a big tackle gave him an elbow on the third play, whiplashing his head and cracking three vertebrae in his neck. Then, while he was lying on the ground, the big man stepped on him and snapped off the end of his coccyx. When the referee came over to see how badly he was hurt, Lulu called him a son of a bitch and bit his hand so the blood came.

Then Jack Lynch came, and everything changed. It was like having Lulu on the team all year long, as big as he *thought* he was.

But it wasn't all silver and gold.

Not in the beginning it wasn't.

# 3

Word about Jack had been out in the town all summer, getting stretched and improved on and amplified.

"New Orleans, man! New Orleans!"

They made it sound like Notre Dame.

"He played ball in New Aw-*leans*!"

In Savannah that was practically the next best thing to Notre Dame itself, especially with the slant that J. J. O'Brien was putting on it. Which was that the New Orleans high schools were like a regular farm system, which Coach Leahy himself spent a lot of time cultivating and worrying about up there in South Bend. That was J. J.'s story, the way he worked it up.

In fact, New Orleans did have some very strong Catholic high school teams back in those days, so the idea didn't altogether drop out of his pants leg.

The interest in football that blew up in Savannah was considerable, but it had to do mostly with high school teams, the reason being that the nearest colleges were a full day's drive away by automobile — the University of Georgia in Athens and Georgia Tech in Atlanta — both up in the northern end of the state and, so to speak, a pretty abstract proposition as far as Chatham County was concerned. The Central of Georgia Railroad had a day train—the *Nancy Hanks*—that made a round trip to Atlanta, going up in the morning and coming back the same night, and some of the college crowd would ride it up to see the Tech-Georgia games, the years they played in Atlanta. But taking that excursion to see football games on a regular basis was limited mostly to doctors and real estate developers and wholesale liquor dealers. The man on the street didn't have the cash. So the average rabid football fan had to develop his conception of the possibilities of the sport out in Grayson Stadium on Friday nights, where the Fighting Irish and the Big Blue of Oglethorpe played their games. Unfortunately, the local teams were terrible, on the average. A good year did come along every now and then, but mostly Savannah football was nothing at all to get inspired about or build a myth on.

There were regular glimpses of what the game might be, which the fans got from the up-country teams that came down to stomp the locals into the ground. And once in a while there would be the good teams, or an isolated Savannah player who would pop up and fulfill their expectations on the legendary side—as Horse Rooney had done in the early forties, playing fullback for Boniface. Those were the ones the fans had to hold onto. Season by season, they mostly had to keep up their faith in football as a game of giants and heroes by sheer unsupported vision and willpower, anchored by believing in teams that were real—that is, teams that were from real places—but so far away nobody ever got to see them. Big Locker Rooms in the Sky, full of mean linemen and snaky backs, who finished their high school days getting scholarships to play football at places like Tennessee and Alabama and Georgia Tech. And even—the sweaty ultimate thought—at Notre Dame itself.

The Atlanta teams showed up in Grayson Stadium once in a while because the Savannah schools would occasionally get on the schedule of Boys' High and Marist, though talking them into it was hard since there wasn't much glory in it for anybody. Whenever they did come down, the Savannah team would get slaughtered, with scores that looked like the odds against the sun's coming up. Especially when they were playing Boys' High. So there was a certain realistic dimension at the root of the Atlanta part of the myth.

Boys' High of Atlanta was good, but, since it was a team that the fans actually did get to see now and then, it never did stir their imaginations in quite the same way as the New Orleans teams, or those of Knoxville and Nashville and Chattanooga. There was never any firsthand contact with those schools, so reality never impinged on the myths and lies. With those faraway teams, the scope of the vision was unconstrained.

There was also a certain kind of reverse mythology that said that the teams from Florida and California were made up of fairies and jelly beans, who spent all their time polishing their fingernails and slicking down their hair. Those states were noted for peripheral things, things just on the edges of the game—cheerleaders who put out, and hundred-member marching bands full of saxophone players with big fannies, and big-bosomed pompom girls. Nothing seemed to make a dent in that particular piece of folklore. Of course, nobody ever got to *see* a team from California, but it wouldn't have made any difference. Jacksonville High School came up to Savannah four years running in the forties and wiped up Grayson Stadium with the Big Blue of Oglethorpe. After they left, the field was gritty with teeth, and the trail of blood to the Big Blue locker room didn't fade out until the baseball crowd walked it away in the middle of the summer. But all the fans ever remembered were the bosoms on the cheerleaders and the fannies on the saxophone players.

"Two thirty, man! Two fucking thirty!"

They liked to talk about his size, but the truth is that the myth never did catch up with reality there.

Jack weighed 240, but even the biggest of the big-mouths were afraid to stretch the story that far. They didn't know how much he weighed really but were building on his playing weight for the 1946 season, which they did know, because J. J. O'Brien had told them. It had been 215, which everybody assumed was a lie in the first place.

But it wasn't. And then Jack had had a growing spurt over the winter, going up an inch in height, to six feet four, and gaining twenty-five pounds. Those were facts that smashed right through the roof of all the allowable standards at the time. And, besides, the ones who were making up the stories didn't have all that much imagination and had to hold closer to reality than is good for really artful lying. The only Savannah player then on the first team of a major college was Leon Hook, who was playing first-string center for Georgia Tech at 175 pounds, and they felt like they had to keep that in mind. In those days a playing weight of more than two hundred pounds had to be sworn to on a Bible and signed by a notary public. Anything over 220 was regarded as an outright lie, just on the face of it. And even then, the really big men usually turned out to be lardasses, like Feeb, who were suited up mostly for the psychological advantage of having their weight listed in the program.

So nobody believed what was being said about Jack. Which should have been an encouragement to work it up bigger and better than ever since that kind of lying is more a matter of entertainment than deception. But 230 was the sticking point, the place where their nerve gave out. Nobody would make the first move to lie it up from there.

Taken all together, J. J. and the alumni were pretty joyful about Jack and what he was going to do for Boniface football. J. J. even played a long shot and mailed a season ticket to the Pope. He never got an answer, of course, but he didn't want to overlook any possibility.

Before every home game he checked the seat—just in case.

But the team—well, the team was another matter. Gloom was the word there. G-L-O-O-M. Black and brooding and in capital letters. Jack's specter clouded their summer like a vulture's wing.

Most of the players knew him, and most liked him well enough. But it wasn't Jack himself so much as the idea of him that was getting them down. He had always spent his summers in Savannah, and several of them had gone to school with him back in the elementary grades, before Kate sent him out of town. But seeing him down at the beach, or at the CYPA, or in Theodore's Ice Cream Parlor was one thing. Dealing with the myth that J. J. and the alumni were cranking out was another. Eventually, the Jack that they knew and the one bagged up in the bigmouth idea of him came together in their minds, collecting in a resentful lump at the top of their spinal columns. They didn't talk about it at all among themselves because they couldn't. It wasn't the kind of thing that could be worked over out in the open. But it darkened their days, making them broody and distant.

All of them knew that having Jack on the team was going to make a very big difference to Boniface. But it was just that difference that hung them up. Every face on the first two teams sagged an inch-and-a-half between June 1 and August 11, which was when practice was scheduled to start. Each of them was working it out on his own, but they were all coming to the same conclusion.

Jack was a winner. He had played three years for teams that didn't lose — or at least for teams that didn't lose as a matter of course the way they did. For that reason, he would be used to winning and would expect Boniface to win, too. So went the sad litany. Well, they wanted that, too — in a way. But the kind of speculation that Jack was stirring up was, after all, a reflection on them. And it caught them just there — between an abstract good, which they had to agree to, and a personal inclination, which they didn't want to admit. A moral dilemma is what it was, and they had to stew in it, each to himself alone, over the whole long summer. What they were locked up about wasn't Jack himself, but J. J.'s version of him, which, as it turned out, was an understatement at that.

So the locker room crowd wasn't all that cheerful when practice started in the summer of 1947. All the regular members of the team were humpbacked and pouty, and sullen as a chain gang. They shuffled into the locker room, taking seats at the back and hunkering down in a constipated kind of way, without looking at each other or at Jack. Ducker rolled his eyes around at them once, then drilled his gaze into the floor at his feet and whispered the universal thought. "I feel like I got a turd wedged sideways."

"Fucking A," somebody said.

\* \* \*

"Well . . ."

Coach Garfield always started his talks with *well*. He did that to avoid starting them with *um*, which he had read somewhere was the mark of a poor speaker. He hated talking to groups—mortally hated it. But books on public speaking had the kind of fascination for him that books on forensic medicine have for certain morbid kinds of people—or illustrated books on cancer. He always had one checked out of the library to lay up on his bedside table and make himself miserable with.

Giving a talk at the first practice session wasn't what he wanted to do at all, and nobody said that he had to do it. But his sense of style wouldn't let him alone. It told him that giving a talk was something that he *ought* to do. When his sense of style didn't tell him that, his sense of obligation did. He felt that he couldn't just send the team out and let them start playing football. There would be something incomplete about it. Chicken's sense of style was all the time getting in the way of his inclinations and causing him trouble.

"Well," he said. He drew it out, "Weelllll . . . I feel pretty . . . good about the team."

"You do?" said Frog.

Being interrupted in the middle of a talk made him lose his place, and he would have to flounder around trying to find it again. When it happened right at the beginning, he just started over. Talking and answering questions were two things he couldn't do at the same time.

"Well . . . ," he said.

Whenever he had to make a talk, he would write it out ahead of time and try to memorize it. But his memory wasn't all that good either, and the speech always got away from him when the time came. What happened was that he tended just to hit the high spots — those being the only parts he could remember. So nothing he said went together, and none of the players ever knew what he was talking about. But it never occurred to any of them to say anything about it. Football coaches were pretty much beyond criticism in those days, except when they were losing. And at Boniface even then.

The team was with him in spirit, and the words didn't matter that much anyway. It was the moment that mattered. They knew him to be a kind and earnest man, and if he thought of anything that would help them improve the team, he would find a way to get it across to them.

"You boys . . . last year . . . I mean . . ." He sighed sadly. "It don't pay to *dwell* on that." He shook his head like a dog with a tick in his ear, then looked around the room, trying for eye contact. "Man for man, you couldn't ask for better . . ." He dropped his eyes to the floor and adjusted something in his crotch. As a sort of reply or acknowledgment, the team adjusted something in their crotches too. "With the schedule we've got . . ." And on and on.

There were ninety-four boys in the locker room, about sixty of them just there for the first day. Boniface usually suited up thirty or so men for the squad, but because of the way they felt about football around the school, there were always three times that many packed into the locker room at the beginning of practice in the fall and in the spring. Most of them would be gone the next day because it was only a gesture in the first place. A few would stick it out for a day or two beyond that. But the first day — ninety-four.

It looked like a mob to Chicken. And the locker room was small anyway. Later, when only the playing squad was left, he would be a little more relaxed. Not much, but some. What he had to say wouldn't make any more sense, but it wouldn't worry him so much. Words were never his strong point.

"Um . . . ," he said.

The ones who were just out for the first day kept trying to follow him and make some kind of sense out of what he was saying, sitting on the edge of the benches and bobbing their heads up and down. After all, it was the only inside look at the game that most of them would ever get, and they wanted to work in as close to the core of the mystery as they could in the short, painless time they were giving up to it.

The real team, the ones who were there for the season, were sitting off toward the back, slouching down. In other years a lot of them would bring funny books to read, and magazines like *Titter*. This year they sat brooding and empty-handed, silent mourners at dejection's black wall.

All except Frog Finnechairo, who had three pieces of Fleer's bubble gum in his mouth and was reading the comic-strip wrappers with a serious look on his face.

"So this year I know we're going to do it," said Chicken. He was skipping the last two paragraphs to get to the punch line, but nobody noticed, of course. Frog had a bubble going that was as big as his head, and most of the players were turned around watching him. Even the first-day boys.

"Now I want you to meet a new man," said Chicken. "Jack Lynch."

When he said that, everybody stopped watching Frog, just as the bubble broke and collapsed on his face.

"Lynch's going to say a few words to you," said Chicken.

"Did you see it?" said Frog, his voice muffled behind the pink membrane of bubble gum that covered his head like a caul.

Jack stood up. He had been sitting behind Coach Garfield during the talk, and when he stood up, at first he didn't look so big. But that was because he seemed to be standing right beside him—which he wasn't. He walked forward three steps, and when he did, it looked like his head was going to go through the ceiling of the locker room.

The trick about it was the way Jack was built. Until he got right up beside something that could act as a reference point, he looked like just an ordinary boy—well built, of course. If you saw him half a block away, cut loose from things you might be able to gauge him by, you would guess he was about five feet eight or nine. Six feet four—that always came as a surprise. Something about him negated the rules of perspective. It was a difficult thing to adjust to.

"You all know me," he said. "Most of you do. This is where I'm from." He didn't like making speeches either, but Coach Garfield thought it would be a good idea. "Just a few words, Jack," he'd said. "Something to start us out." He had begun laying things off on Jack right away.

"We can have a good team." His way of talking was downright, but his voice was high for such a big man. High, with just a touch of hoarseness in it. Tenors ran in his family.

"Louder, Lynch." Ducker's voice was flat. He had stood up and was leaning against the wall at the back with his arms folded, hugging himself.

Jack looked at him for a minute, then went on. "We can have a good team," he said. "But we've got to hustle."

"You got to talk *louder*, Lynch," said Ducker.

"I think we'll have a good team," said Jack, without raising his voice. He pulled his nose with his thumb and first finger, then looked at Coach Garfield. "That's all I've got to say, Coach."

Chicken looked a little surprised. "That's all?"

"Yes," said Jack. "I think . . . you know. We can have a good team."

"Well . . . ," said Chicken. "Okay . . ." He fiddled with his whistle, then put his stern look on. "Hit the field, men," he said.

For a minute Jack looked at Ducker, his head tilted a little to one side. Then he put on his helmet and went out of the locker room. The one-day boys followed. And then the team. All except Frog, who was blowing a bubble at the time. He pinched it closed with his lips and took it out of his mouth.

"Look!" he said to the empty locker room.

"How can you eat *two* of those things?" said Jack.

He and Feeb had stopped by Theodore's after practice on Tuesday, and Feeb was finishing his second hot fudge sundae. Jack was drinking a Coke.

"Wipe your mouth," said Jack, handing Feeb a napkin across the booth. Feeb took it and smeared the fudge around his mouth.

"Do it again," said Jack, handing him another napkin. "You go after that thing like it was a piece of pussy."

Of all the people on the team, Feeb was the one that Jack knew the best. The Siddoneys lived on Lincoln Street, just around the corner from the Lynch house on Waldburg. He and Jack had gone to grade school together.

Jack took the straw out of his cup and started eating the ice, tapping the bottom with his finger. "We got no hustle," he said.

Feeb was lifting a big spoonful of sundae to his

mouth. He stopped and looked at Jack. While he was doing it, a long string of fudge sagged out of the spoon and into his lap. Feeb didn't notice. "Man," he said, "you got to be kidding." Then he shot the spoon into his mouth.

"No hustle. No drive," said Jack. "Everybody's dragging ass."

Feeb rammed another spoonful of ice cream and fudge into his mouth. "You think it's going to make a difference?"

"You don't hustle, you don't win," said Jack.

"Boniface don't win anyway," said Feeb. "Hustle or no hustle."

"That's the way we're acting," said Jack. "Everybody is acting that way."

"Ever . . ." Feeb had a big spoonful of sundae in his mouth, and when he tried to talk, fudge ran out of the corners. He worked it around to the side. "Everybody *is* that way," said Feeb. "That's the fucking score, Jack. Everybody knows it. Everybody knows the motherfucker."

"You've got to hustle," said Jack. "You've got to want to do it."

"This ain't New Orleans," said Feeb. He reamed the sides of the sundae dish with his spoon, then licked it twice on each side. "It's hanging over from last year. The whole first team. We didn't lose a man."

Jack handed him another napkin. "I got beat twice in the last three years," he said.

Feeb looked at him over the napkin. "Twice?" He wiped his mouth. "Jesus. Get a grip on your ass."

"I hate to lose," said Jack.

"You get used to it."

"No you don't," said Jack. "I wouldn't get used to it worth a damn."

Feeb ran the spoon around the sundae dish again. "It ain't so bad, once you get used to it."

"You beat Kose," said Jack. "I know how you did last year."

"So you know what I'm talking about?"

"You beat Kose High School," said Jack.

Feeb looked at him. "Kose is a Class-C school," he said. "They've got a hundred and sixty-eight students. Total."

"You came close to beating Glynn Academy."

"We wasn't hustling," said Feeb. "There was a flu epidemic in Brunswick. They had nine players in the hospital."

"Don't you give a shit?" said Jack.

Feeb looked at him, then scraped the spoon in the dish and licked it. "Not particularly," he said. "We hustled at the first of the year. We still got our ass beat." He jiggled the spoon. "Fuck it," he said and dropped the spoon into the dish.

"You're giving me the redass, Feeb."

"Three games in four years, man. *Four* years. Even with the Pope on our side. Go talk to my old man. He burned fifty candles last fall. You got to know where you stand, man."

"*You've* got something to do with where you stand," said Jack.

Feeb looked up at him, but he didn't say anything.

"Boniface had some good teams back during the war."

"All the heroes got killed," said Feeb. "They all got their ass shot off."

"Horse Rooney is still around."

"*Three* motherfucking games, man," said Feeb. "You going to get beer out of horse piss sooner than you get a winner out of that bunch."

Jack crunched on his ice and Feeb ordered another sundae.

"What's Hoy's trouble? Is it me?"

"You know," said Feeb, digging into the sundae. "He's the bigshot tackle."

"You weigh more than he does," said Jack.

Feeb rolled his eyes. "Come *on*, man," he said. "You know what I fucking mean. He wants to beat your ass. He's not sure how it'd come out."

"Hoy's a battler. He wouldn't be scared of me."

"He can't handle you playing football," said Feeb. "You don't know the talk we been hearing all summer." He took another scoop of ice cream. "They made you sound like King Kong with a hard-on. It kind of made *me* hate your guts even."

"Okay," said Jack. He stood up.

"Hey, man," said Feeb. "Manner of speaking. I didn't mean that."

"I know," said Jack. "I've got to go."

"Where you going?"

"I need a brew," said Jack. "I want to think about it."

"Breaking fucking training," said Feeb. "That's the spirit." He scraped the sides of his sundae dish.

"Think I should talk to him about it? Hoy?"

"No," said Feeb. "Beat his ass. It'll do him good."

Jack started out the door.

"Wait a minute," said Feeb, squeezing out of the booth. "I'll go with you."

"You going to drink *beer* on top of that?"

"Sure," said Feeb, a surprised look on his face. "Something wrong with that?"

"Wipe your face," said Jack.

"I want you to put me one-on-one against Hoy." It was Monday of the second week, the first day of contact, and Jack had taken Coach Garfield aside to speak to him.

Chicken looked at Jack, surprised. "Let it go," he said. "Hoy's the best lineman I've got, next to you. I can't afford to have you busting each other up."

"Nobody's going to get busted up," said Jack. "Just put us one-on-one."

Chicken looked at him and fiddled with his whistle.

"You want to straighten out this team?" said Jack.

"I need the both of you," said Chicken.

"I know you do," said Jack. "Do what I'm telling you."

It evened out. Jack was bigger than Ducker, but Ducker was meaner. And Ducker was big too. Even Jack didn't have enough size just to power him around any way he wanted to. But Ducker didn't understand the fine points of the game as well as Jack did. So he spent the first half-hour of practice on his backside. By the time the drill was over, Ducker's face looked like a tomato. When they thought Ducker wasn't looking, some of the B-team players smiled at the way Jack was handling him. Ducker had caught it and it made him try harder, but Jack was too quick for him to get a solid shot at. He finally lost his temper altogether and swung on Jack. He split Jack's helmet. Coach Garfield saw it and came over and broke it up. "I need the both of you," he said.

"I want to see you a minute after you get dressed, Hoy," said Jack. "Under the goalpost."

Ducker looked at him and spit on the ground. "Any place you say, Lynch," he said.

After he got dressed, Jack went out and stood under the goalpost, waiting for Ducker to come out.

"Stay right there, Hoy," said Jack, holding out his hand. Ducker was ten feet away from him. There was a dead look on his face, and his fists were clenched. "Hard to beat your ass from here, Lynch."

"Got a mind to do that, have you, Hoy? Well, I'll give you a shot at it."

"What?" said Ducker. "I got a bad ear. Talk louder."

"You broke my helmet. How's your hand?"

"Good enough."

"You're going to have to wait, Hoy. I'll give you a shot after the season's over."

Ducker looked at him.

"That's what I wanted to talk to you about," said Jack. His hands were resting on his hips lightly. "Stash it away, Hoy. Hoard it up. When we're through with the football, I'll give you a chance."

Ducker looked at him. "I never liked putting things off, Lynch. Do it while the doing's good."

"You can't win, Hoy."

"What?" said Ducker. "What?"

"You'll have to cripple me. You may beat my ass, but you won't enjoy it. You'll have to beat the shit out of me. How's that for the team?"

Ducker looked at him, frowning.

"I was just fucking around out there today," said Jack. "You ought to see what I can do when I put my *mind* to it."

Ducker was the best street battler in the school. That's what everyone said. A different proposition. Not like football. He had never been known to lose a fight, and he picked them with *everybody*. Sailors off the ships that came into the Port Authority. Soldiers up from Camp Stewart. Even Marines fresh out of boot camp at Parris Island. He was also the heavyweight on the boxing team. Just something he liked to do.

"You got no choice, Hoy. Friday after Thanksgiving. I'll meet you down at Screven. Anyplace you want to." He stopped. "I'm not looking forward to it," he said. Then he paused. "I'll meet you anyplace you want to."

Ducker knew he was trapped. He couldn't cripple Jack and take him off the team, but he also couldn't handle him at practice.

"God *damn* it, Lynch."

"You see how it is?"

"Yeah. Shit yeah." Ducker looked at the ground and kicked it with his heel. "You pushed me around too goddamn much today, Lynch. Don't nobody get to do that."

"I pushed you around because I'm better than you are," said Jack. Then he added, "At football." He paused a minute. "Coach Garfield needs the both of us. You're the only decent lineman we've got. You and Chippy Depeau."

"Pushed me around . . ."

"You're big enough to handle me better than that."

"I ain't had your big-time advantages, Lynch. I never even *been* to New Orleans."

"Get on the team, Hoy. We need you. I'll meet you Friday after Thanksgiving at Fort Screven. Anyplace you say."

"Who the fuck you think you are, Lynch? Pushing me around like that?"

"You should be handling me better than you were."

Ducker looked at him, thinking. He spit on the ground.

"You like to lose, Hoy?"

"No," said Ducker. "I don't fucking like to lose." He thought a minute. "I don't fucking like to get pushed around either."

"Get on the team," said Jack.

"Lynch . . . ," said Ducker, pointing his finger at Jack. For a minute they stood looking at each other without saying anything.

"You want me to show you what you were doing wrong?" said Jack.

When the word got out in the school about Jack's deal with Ducker, the bookmaking began right away. They were tough odds to figure, and never were settled in a permanent way.

Jack was big in the bone, probably weighing forty-five pounds more than Ducker did, but taller and trimmer. He carried his weight well, and most of his agility was in his legs. Ducker was on the flat-footed side. His speed was in his hands, which made him a good battler, but it wasn't of much use to him on the football field. He was a very good boxer. In the ring he didn't have to depend on anyone else, which he liked. Jack was a wrestler.

In a fist fight, Jack's weight wasn't all that much of an advantage. After all, Ducker weighed about as much as Dempsey had. And Joe Louis had come near beating

Primo Carnera to death. The Italian was even bigger than Jack.

The odds were running about four-and-a-half to five—in Ducker's favor since Jack was the unknown quantity. But those were talking odds. There wasn't any money being bet.

Although the interests of the school didn't lie over that way, everybody would have liked to see the two big men go ahead and have their fight. It was more basic than football.

But, in the meantime, Ducker got on the team.

As he said, he didn't like losing all that much either.

Having Jack and Ducker together went a long way toward getting the eleven men moving as a unit, but that didn't mean all the problems had been solved.

Since his play was going to be in the interior line, the line was Jack's first consideration. He wanted two good guards and at least one good tackle. Feeb he more or less wrote off, having known him all his life. Everything Feeb did struck him as comical, and he couldn't take him seriously enough to work with him. He thought they could survive one weak link, if everybody else would hustle.

The first step was to get everybody's mind off himself, so he could see what was going on around him—after which they would be able to forget it.

To do that, he suggested to Coach Garfield that one day they swap around on the linemen's positions. So they did a round robin, every man taking a turn at each position from tackle to tackle, trying to get a feel for what the others were doing. Seeing how their part fit into the pattern. In the end, they began to trust each other, so they didn't have to cover a 360-degree field in their heads to feel safe.

The ends and backs were something else again. Whistler Whitfield and Cowboy McGrath were unknown quantities since they had never had a line to block for them before and weren't used to getting *through* their holes. Breaking out on the downfield side of the line was a new experience for them and did a whole lot for their morale just by itself.

Flasher, Aaron, and Dimmy were the real mountains to be moved. Frog—well, with Frog the dimension of the problem was different. There wasn't any real hope of doing anything through his head. With Frog they had to work from the outside in. Well, as far in as they could get.

To take care of Frog's sense of direction, the times he would get turned around, they kept up the Stop Frog drills. Jack solved the problem of Frog's being short on yardage by detailing two managers, one on each side of the field, to mark the down by blinking a flashlight so it would attract Frog's attention and show him where to go. The flashlights had green lenses, which they thought the officials would take for some kind of spirit thing because of the color. They didn't expect them to complain. Frog wanted the lights to be red, but they reminded him that the school colors were *green* and white, which would make the green light easier to explain to the officials if they ever had to.

"Red is my *favorite* color," said Frog.

Jack told Aaron to stop fading back so far. And when he kept on doing it, he had a talk with him about it.

"You don't need to go back there so far, Aaron. You're not getting the best out of your arm."

"I like to have room to move around," said Aaron.

"But you're not getting the best out of your arm."

Aaron didn't want to argue with him about it. "I like to move around back there, Lynch," he said.

"You can get it out there pretty good, Aaron," said Jack, "but you're losing accuracy. Don't drop back more than ten yards. We're going to be blocking for you."

It was like talking down a posthole. Aaron went right on running for the goal line, his own, as soon as he had snatched the ball from Jack. Just like he always had.

"Stop fading back so far, Aaron," said Jack. "I'm telling you, you're using up your arm just getting back to the line."

"One man calling signals, Lynch," said Aaron. "One man calling signals."

"Goddamn it, Bomberstern, you don't need to run out of the stadium."

Aaron looked at him for a minute without saying anything. "Fuck you," he said.

He kept fading back his twenty and thirty yards, with Jack complaining at him after every play. Finally Jack turned around and chased him all the way into the end zone, where Aaron threw the ball away and climbed the goalpost. "One man calling signals, Lynch," he said, looking down from the crossbar.

"You're going to stop doing it, Aaron." Jack looked up at him and shook his finger. "I promise you."

He called the guards and halfbacks aside and had a private talk with them about Aaron's bad habits. "We've got to harass him," he said. "If he fades back more than fifteen yards, whoever is back there blocking has got to nail him."

"You mean tackle him?" said Bo Hoerner.

"I wasn't thinking of anything that showy," said Jack.

"Our *own* man?" said Bo.

"He's too much out for himself," said Jack. "We've got to get him thinking for the team. He can't expect us to block for him if he's out for himself."

"I don't like it," said Bo.

"I like it fine," said Whistler Whitfield. "The son of a bitch ain't given me a good hand-off in the last two years."

"We'll work on that next," said Jack. "First we've got to stop him running out of the stadium."

Jack showed them how to do it. On the first pass play, he backed up with Aaron, and when he started to break and run for the goal line, Jack hit him. He did it well, so that it looked like an accident, but he drew blood on Aaron's leg.

"Look!" said Aaron. "Look at the blood! Goddamn watch where you're going, Lynch." There was true anguish in Aaron's voice.

"I was trying to keep up with you, Aaron," said Jack. "Stay up closer to the line."

"Look at my leg," said Aaron. "It's *bleeding*! Look at me bleeding on my leg."

They had to hold up practice while Aaron went into the locker room and put a bandage on the scratch.

The next turn was Whistler Whitfield's. He didn't make it look as good as Jack did, but, then, he had more to make up for. He didn't make it look deliberate either.

"Goddamn, Whitfield," said Aaron. "Goddamn, goddamn, goddamn."

"Sorry," said Whistler. There was a smile on his face.

Aaron went into the locker room, and they had to wait for him while he put on another bandage. The knocks they were giving him made him bitch and carry on, but, little by little, he began to unload the ball faster, just to avoid being hurt.

"It makes sense," said Jack. "By the time Aaron can make ten, Flasher can make thirty. And, besides, Flasher won't have all that time to fool around out there."

The next thing was to get Aaron using more deception in his hand-offs. Whistler and Cowboy had both been asking Jack to get to that problem right along, but he didn't want to push Aaron too much at once. "One thing at a time," he said. "One thing at a time."

"Easy for you to say," said Whistler.

After he got the fading back under control, Jack took up the problem of Aaron's ball handling.

"Goddamn, Lynch, don't I do *anything* to please you?" said Aaron. "Lujack doesn't hide the ball."

"What the shit do you mean?" said Jack. "Lujack is an ace ball handler."

Aaron looked at him. "He is?" he said.

"You ever seen any game films of Lujack?"

"I've seen him in the newsreels."

"He has a nice touch," said Jack. "Nobody knows who's got the ball when Lujack is handling it."

"Well," said Aaron.

It didn't break him. He just began to look around for some other quarterback who handled the ball according to the way he thought it ought to be done.

"What're we going to do?" said Whistler. "By the time I get the ball, everybody in the fucking stadium knows where it's at, including the janitors in the washroom."

"He's out for himself again," said Jack. "Let's put him on his own. We've got to work with his self-interest just to get his attention."

"Okay," said Whistler. Then he thought a minute. "What the shit does that mean?"

"When you don't like the hand-off . . . don't take it."

"What?"

"I said don't take it," said Jack. "Stick him with the ball."

"Yes," said Whistler and smiled. "Stick him with the ball. I like the way that sounds." He said it again. "Stick him with the ball."

"Just go down in your blocking stance and let him eat it," said Jack. "Aaron won't keep up anything if he gets hurt doing it. We just have to make it in his own interest to hide the thing."

So Whistler and Cowboy stopped taking the ball.

"Take it! Take it!" That was Aaron—terror-stricken—with his arm stretched out behind him, like he was trying to feed a snake, waiting for Whistler to take the ball and let him get out of the way.

"Hide it," said Whistler over his shoulder.

"What the fuck, Whitfield?" said Aaron. Then the two B-team guards nailed him.

"You try to give it to me on a stick, and you can eat it," said Whistler.

"What?" said Aaron, looking at the cut on his arm.

"It's a new day, Bomberstern." Whistler tapped him on the helmet. "We're going to have us a *team*."

They didn't get rid of Aaron's bad habits altogether, but they cut them down to a point where they could live with them. At least they got him to paying attention and seeing their side of the problem.

Jack tried to reason with Flasher and Dimmy, but there wasn't any way to get through to either of them with just words and ideas. Especially Dimmy.

With Aaron getting the ball off faster, part of the problem with Flasher solved itself since he didn't have that much time to fool around after he got downfield and had to pay more attention to what he was doing.

But just for insurance they began to work him over to slow him down off the line—just a little. Jack would give him a heel on the instep coming out of the huddle. Then Ducker picked it up and started to sideswipe him coming off the line. They also got Whistler lining up behind him and telling him things like his fly was open, or his pants were ripped, to attract his attention just before the ball was snapped. They didn't want to interfere with him too much because basically what he was doing was the right thing, though they wished his hands would improve. To help that, they gave him a rosin bag to hang on his pants and made him carry a football around school during the day so he would get to recognize what one felt like. Even so, every third pass to him still bounced off.

Talking to Dimmy was not only a waste of time but could also be harmful. Too many words coming towards him at once seemed to clog him up and slow down his thinking—which wasn't much faster than a duckbill platypus's to start with. They didn't want to get him moody, or too attentive, but they did want him to look where he was going. So Jack and Ducker started pulling off the line and double-teaming him when he was going off guard. They hurt themselves about as much as they hurt Dimmy, but it surprised him and got him to pull his head up just out of curiosity. Being able to see where he was going made him notice that some of his own men were out there in front of him, too, and stopped him from plowing into his own blockers from the back side and walking around on their vertebrae. Which improved their outlook considerably.

Two weeks into practice, the usual lethargy was gone. Everyone was attentive and alert. Well, relatively. Things weren't A-1, letter perfect, but they were silver and gold to what they had been before. A sense of how well everybody else was doing his job began to filter in under the helmets—even Dimmy's. The big thing was that they began to trust each other. Where they had all had a 360-degree field of apprehension before, the new attitude had cut it down to the thirty or forty degrees that was the responsibility of each particular position. That alone meant an improvement of over 900 percent. Of course, some improvements were more important than others. Just getting Dimmy to run with his head up accounted for 300 percent of the improvement all by itself.

They were coming up on the first real test, which took place just before the season opened. The traditional varsity-alumni game.

Every year, on the Saturday afternoon before the season started, the Boniface varsity had to gird up what loins it had and take on the alumni in a real game, which was no pantywaist affair, but a real knock-head session, where bright red blood was expected to flow. There were four twelve-minute quarters, with referees, and full equipment for the players. It never occurred to anyone who came to watch or play in the game that crippling the team might not be the best way to start them out for the season. Football, as they said, was a rough game.

Most of the alumni who turned up to play were out to get back a piece of the glory they had had two or three, some even eight or nine, years before. Taking it easy on the team was the farthest thing from their minds and never came in as part of their view of the game. If the old guys had been able to go flat out for the full four quarters, nobody would have walked away from it whole. But half a game was about the most they could ever bring off. Partly that was because of the way J. J. O'Brien underwrote it—which may have been a calculated thing on his part. J. J. was a sport, but he was a smart one.

The bench on the alumni side of the field was a row of green canvas camp chairs, and there were little Negro boys to run up and down the line delivering pitchers of cold beer and cigars to the players, all supplied by J. J. himself. By the end of the first half, the beer and cigars would be coming down on the alumni pretty heavily, so the second half wasn't much more than a shoving contest, except for the varsity trying to get even for the punishment they had taken in the first half.

But the first twelve minutes were pure bloody murder.

The alumni weren't in very good shape—even without the beer and cigars they weren't. But their mad-dog outlook and their grown-man size made them a rough proposition for a high school team to take on. They outweighed the varsity twenty or thirty pounds to the man, and with that second moment of glory into them the way it was, they were like a herd of wild elephants until their wind gave out.

Usually the game was bad news for somebody in particular on the varsity squad. The whole idea of the game was crazy as hell anyway, but the height of all the craziness was that the alumni concentrated on the best players, trying to maim and disable them in particular. If one of them had a better reputation than the rest, it was a sure thing he would be the one they would focus their attention on. Cutting him down to size gave a focus to the contest. It made things more interesting for the alumni.

In 1947, it was Jack Lynch, of course. And the man to put the test on him was Horse Rooney, the All-State fullback from the 1942 championship team—the one that had beaten Boys' High of Atlanta.

Horse was as mean a snake as ever pulled a green jersey over his head, and as big a one as well. He had made the first team at Boniface in 1939 as a thirteen-year-old freshman at a playing weight of 185. He attracted the coach's attention by breaking the collarbone of the first-string guard during a practice scrimmage. His senior year he weighed 215, and there weren't eleven high school players in the state who could stop him in less than five yards. For the four years since his graduation, Horse had had his natural snaky instincts honed up for him by the United States Marine Corps, which had put thirty more pounds of meat on him and then taught him eleven ways to kill a man with his bare hands. He wasn't in tiptop shape, but he figured to maim about four or five linemen before his wind gave out. Starting with Jack Lynch.

Like most high school teams of the time—college teams too, for the most part—Boniface had two defensive formations. They had a five-man line, and then they had a six-man line. Coach Garfield was going with the five-man line as a regular thing since that would put Jack in the middle and let him move where he needed to from there. Anything between tackles would be his, with Dimmy on the left to help him and Ducker on the right. On Flasher's side of the field, because he could get out fast enough to turn his man in, the end sweeps would also be Jack's. His lateral movement was very good, and he was quick, if not fast. He could almost keep up with Flasher himself for the first ten yards.

The strategy of the alumni was simple and direct. They didn't discuss it until they showed up for the game, and Horse was setting the tone. What he wanted was to get the ball on the first play from scrimmage and go straight up the middle with it, head-on at Lynch. Since that was what everyone wanted to see, there was general agreement they should get on with it right away.

"Just get them other cocksuckers out the way," said Horse, chewing on the stub of his cigar. "It's me and Lynch, boys. Me and Lynch." Then he slapped his hands together, and the skull session was over.

The alumni won the toss with a two-headed coin, and the varsity kicked off to them. It was a short kick, taken by the deep man on the twenty-five. He bobbled it, and Bump Waddell, a twenty-eight-year-old guard from the 1937 team, fell on it at the forty-five-yard line. They didn't bother to huddle but lined up right away, with Horse straight back behind the center. Before they got down into their stances, Horse raised his arm and pointed his finger at Jack.

"Off on three, Lynch," he said. "Watch your ass."

All of the Boniface linemen turned around and looked at Jack. He had his hands on his knees and was looking down at the ground. Then the signals started and the center hiked the ball.

The charge of the alumni line wasn't all that hard. It was a big moment. Everybody knew what was going to happen anyway, and all of them wanted to see it so they would be able to tell about it afterward.

The alumni pushed off right and left, and the varsity backed off the line, checking. Then everyone stood up and turned around to watch Jack and Horse come together in the middle of the thirty-foot hole that had opened up in the center of the field.

Horse ran a good bit like Dimmy, only with his head up more and looking around, his knees pumping against his chest. He had a quick start and was going flat out on the second step he took. But Jack had the faster reflexes, and they came together on the alumni side of the line.

Talking about it afterward, everybody who was there to see it put it in terms of the way they'd felt seeing the newsreel pictures of the atom bomb going off in Alamogordo, New Mexico.

Jack took him high, getting his right shoulder pad into Horse's face and wrapping his arms around him on the outside. Jack never broke stride. There was just a big, cracking sound, like a field piece going off, then the two of them were moving away toward the alumni goal line. Horse's head was buried in Jack's shoulder, and both his legs were sticking out under Jack's arms. The impact split the center seam on Horse's helmet and flipped it off his head backwards so it hung on his neck by the chin strap, like a Mexican bandit's sombrero. And his shoulder pads flapped up out of his jersey like the wings on a beetle.

Jack set him down gently on the forty-two-yard line and stood looking at him with his hands on his hips. Then he looked back at the other players. No one moved or said anything. They were staring at him, some with their mouths hanging open, jumping their eyes up and down from Jack to Horse and back again.

With everybody watching him, he walked back down the middle of the field to where the ball was, on the varsity thirty-five-yard line, moving very slowly and deliberately the whole way. When he got to the ball, he put his foot on it. Then he reached down and tapped it with his hand.

"Our ball," he said.

As soon as he said it, the referee remembered and blew his whistle.

Right away the first-aid squad came onto the field and started to work on Horse, but it took a minute and a half of swatting him on the back to beat the first breath into him, and ten more of breaking ammonia ampoules under his nose and pouring beer on his head to get his eyes uncrossed and his mouth working right.

"How do you feel, Horse?" J. J. yelled it into his ear fifty or sixty times. In between, he would spread out his arms to push back the crowd, chewing on his cigar and yelling, "Give him air, boys! Goddamn it, give him air!"

When Horse's voice started to work back up into his throat again, all he could say was "*God*damn!" over and over.

J. J. stood over him, patting his shoulder and telling him he was going to be all right.

Finally Horse looked up at him in a way that showed he recognized who J. J. was. Then he blinked his eyes and crossed himself. "Goddamn, J. J.!" he said. He made a sucking motion with his lips, working his mouth, then spit out a big, yellow tooth. He smiled up at J. J. through the gap. "Goddamn, J. J.," he said. "We going to have us a *team*!"

# 4

Jack came back to Savannah because his mother wanted him to and because J. J. O'Brien was footing the bill and also because he was homesick in general. But the most intense and cogent of all his reasons, the one that pulled him hardest, was Mary Janone O'Dell—his true and perfect love. Savannah was the place wherein Mary resided, lived, and dwelled.

Their paths had crossed at a house party in the spring of 1946. He saw her first on Friday, leaning against the railing on the Pavilion at Tybee Beach, with the wind in her hair, and a full moon rising yellow out of the ocean behind her.

On Saturday night he took her to Isle of Hope. When they got there, he drove around the bluff and parked at Ballabee's Pavilion. Ballabee's was a special place to him, and he needed to share it with her.

Isle of Hope was ten miles out of town, on the waterfront. The Isle of Hope River was not a river, really, but a tidal estuary. It made a long, brown curve, sweeping against the crescent of a high bluff, going from north to south. Along the bluff a narrow road followed the sweep of the curve, open to the water and marsh on the river side, with a one-deep string of houses on the other. The front yards were long and wide, but in the back, second-growth pines crowded in close, with here and there an outbuilding, or a Negro shanty pushing up against the big main houses that fronted on the bluff.

It was a wonderfully romantic place. The houses were slightly seedy, in a genteel kind of way. Most of them had been built in the last part of the nineteenth century and were occupied by the grandsons and granddaughters of the builders. They were not all alike — the houses — with individual patterns in the crenellations and towers. Some had widow's walks, and some did not. But they had all come out of the same basic conception of style — solid and fancy.

They were all big, two-story, clapboard-sided, and mostly white — with wide, screened porches wrapping them around on the front and sides. From the high front steps, oystershell walks led down to the road, and across to docks and boathouses hanging on the bluff on the river side.

Midway between the horns of the crescent was Ballabee's Pavilion and Turtle Farm — the only commercial establishment on the island. There was not even a grocery store.

In the early 1900s, Ballabee's had been a thriving place, with dances every weekend, played for by Blue Steele and Tony Pastor and other well-known bands of the time. Excursion boats left on Sundays for trips to Beaufort and Tybee Island and Wassaw. A streetcar line ran out from Savannah, and townspeople would rattle out on it to spend Sundays and holidays in the summer, drinking beer and cooled lemonade in the afternoons under the roof of the pavilion, while the Chatham Artillery Band played the kind of heart-raising music that had been popular then — Strauss waltzes and marches by John Philip Sousa. Then, after the sun went down, there would be dancing by the light of Japanese lanterns to songs like "My Gal Sal" and "The Bowery" and "After the Ball."

For Isle of Hope and Ballabee's the high point had come during the Grand Prix races in 1910 and 1911. Ballabee himself had worked for the Fiat team as a mechanic, and many of the drivers were put up at the houses along the bluff, taken in as guests by the families. Every night everyone would be down at the pavilion, the drivers bellied up to the bar, some wearing their helmets with the goggles pushed up on top, smoking black, hand-rolled cigars and talking about the trial heats in languages that rattled and hissed and grunted, or in halting, twisty-mouthed English. Barney Oldfield had been there, and Carlos Fellini, and Eric Steiner, who was driving for the Dusenbergs. The center of gravity of the whole town had shifted out to Ballabee's for the spring, with four extra cars running in tandem on the streetcar line, and a band every night, and crowds on the pier that swayed the pilings and made them groan, sinking them deeper into the mud under the bluff.

But in the years after World War II, Ballabee's had fallen into decline. Even the turtle farm had lost its momentum. In a way, James — the current Ballabee — was trying to keep up with the times.

There was a soda fountain and a gallery of pinball machines at the entrance, but the pavilion itself — the dance floor and the bandstand hanging over the river — that was graying out in the wind and weather. The profit margin on dances was too small and chancy, and James didn't think it justified the initial investment to fix things up. All the paint had peeled off the railings and benches, and the wood had gone powdery and velvet to the touch.

James, who was the grandson of the Ballabee who had built the pavilion, seemed to lack the gay and festive spirit of his father and grandfather. No daring. And, anyway, dance bands weren't his style. A jukebox was. With colored lights bubbling in the tubes and a clear and certain profit of a nickle on every song played.

Except for the first ten feet from the entrance, where a small amount of cash came over the counter from the pinball machines and the soda fountain, James didn't pay any attention to the pavilion at all. Only the Wurlitzer.

The concessions were fenced off and locked at night behind metal grilles, to protect the pinball machines. But he left the main part of the pier, the dance floor, open since he didn't care about it anyway, and there wasn't anything that could happen to it. The jukebox was unplugged, and there was a locked metal grille around it as well.

Now and then one of the locals would wander down and drop a crab line off the floating dock or set some baskets. Nobody came out from town anymore. The streetcar didn't run. At night the pier was deserted, even in the summertime, and Jack liked to go there and stand looking down into the water when he had things on his mind. It had just the right degree of loneliness—a deserted public place—with echoes of the other times in the loft over the dance floor to keep him company. Occasionally he would see a shark winding around the pilings down below.

Jack and Mary walked out to the end of the dance floor, then down the ramp to the floating dock. The tide was on the ebb, and the eddies around the pilings made sucking noises, like water going down a drain. Streetlights at each side of the entrance on the bluff lit up the sign-plastered clapboard, casting shadows of the railing onto the old dance floor and out over the water. There were boats moored at the south end of the bluff, and their riding lights made a small, fallen constellation in the darkness, bobbing with the movement of the water.

It was at this time and in this place that Jack first held Mary and kissed her and told her he loved her. He vowed to himself he would love her forever, and, since he was sixteen, a vow to himself was a serious matter.

By Sunday night he had worked her up into a niche from which he was never able to let her climb down. Mary was no fool, and she discovered right away that she liked the niche. Being adored had many appealing aspects, and she adored Jack in return for the feeling he generated in her.

It was still possible in those days — that kind of romantic worship of a certain fragile sort of girl. In the movies it happened regularly to women like Madeleine Carroll and Olivia de Havilland. It wasn't an especially healthy attitude because disappointment for one or both of the parties was a very likely thing down the line. But it was pretty common just the same.

Everybody noticed the way Jack was feeling about Mary, but it bothered Feeb.

"Just think about her dropping her drawers and taking a great big shit," said Feeb.

His motives were good — at least about as good as they ever got — since he was trying to swing Jack back into reality, the way he saw it, but the point didn't get home, and Jack hit him. It was one of the few times he ever took Feeb seriously.

"Shit, man," said Feeb. "Motherfucker." He rubbed his eye.

Afterward, Jack told him not to say it again, feeling sorry but at the same time justified. Later he was the one who drove Feeb to the emergency room of the hospital.

* * *

It had been a bad weekend for Feeb all around. The girls were doing their own cooking, so the food was lousy. And all of the regular eating places were closed because the season didn't start until Memorial Day. There wasn't a hot fudge sundae to be had on the whole island, and the only decent hamburger was fifteen miles away back in town. But his date turned out to be the biggest problem of all.

Feeb was out with Corinne Feliciano, a small, dark-haired girl with big brown eyes — and a peculiarity that was the subject of a whole lot of talk among the boys at Boniface. The thing about Corinne was that she never wore underwear when she went out with boys. Never. And she liked to get her date to roll up his pants leg so she could straddle his shin and ride it like a hobbyhorse. As a way to begin an evening, that would have been okay. But the trouble was the bareback riding never got any further along than that. Nobody ever laid a finger on Corinne, and she was always surprised and indignant and loudmouthed about it whenever anybody tried. Corinne had a lot of first dates because the whole thing sounded very interesting — before the boy got into it, with her up there humping on his leg, then screaming bloody murder when he made the first false move — but the repeat business was very slow. There was just too much frustration involved. Though there was also a certain amount of challenge to taking her out.

Feeb knew all about it, but he had a secret plan to beat the game. He had gotten some inside information from Whistler Whitfield that he thought was going to make him the man to knock off Corinne Feliciano.

Whistler was acknowledged to be the biggest cocksman at Boniface, if not in the world, and whatever he had to say about women received careful attention. He didn't talk about it all that much as a rule, but Feeb had asked him a direct question.

Whistler was a pretty serious-minded kind of person in general, but when he spoke about sexual congress with women, his manner developed a dimension which bordered on the theological. "The surest way . . . ," he said, ". . . ain't no way *sure*, but the surest way I know, is to lay your joint in her hand."

Feeb looked at him. "What do you mean?" he said.

"I mean what I'm fucking saying, man," said Whistler. He held out his left hand, palm up, and hit it with his right. "Lay it in her goddamn hand."

Feeb looked at Whistler's hand, his head shaking from side to side.

"Listen," said Whistler, "women ain't much on looking, but put it in their *hand* . . . ," he nodded his head, ". . . they'll cream in their jeans every time. *Feeling* is something else again. Besides," he said, "it's bassackwards to what they're expecting. What they're expecting is that you'll be trying to get the old finger up the tube. Turning it around on them like that throws the shit out of them." Though Whistler's manner was theological, his vocabulary was secular to the maximum.

"I'll be goddamned," said Feeb. "You mean put it in her *hand*?"

"Feeb," said Whistler, smiling and speaking with his eyes closed, "I'm telling you about the golden legspreader. The pussyville express. Get it out and lay her hand on it. You won't know what hit your ass."

"I be goddamned," said Feeb.

Whistler never did say specifically that Corinne Feliciano was going to respond like that, but the way Feeb figured it, a woman was a woman. And the part about their liking to feel more than look had a scientific ring to him.

So that's what he tried.

It took a long time to get Corinne's hand pried off, even with three of them working on her. Feeb wasn't moving at all, just sitting there on the backseat of Jack's DeSoto with his eyes rolled up in his head and his fingernails dug into the upholstery. But the moans he was letting out put everybody's nerves on edge and slowed down the work. Corinne never made a sound, just sat there staring straight ahead while they peeled her fingers loose one at a time.

"I thought we were going to have to wait for the sun to go down to get her to turn loose," said Jack on the way to the hospital. "Or cut off her head like a snapping turtle."

"She sure had a grip on her," said Whistler. "For such a little girl."

The place where she had been hanging on was mashed and ropy-looking, but the other end was all swollen up like a balloon, and about the shade of purple of a damson plum. With Feeb holding it in his hand to protect it, it looked like a ball-ended watch fob.

"I hate to tell you, old buddy," said Whistler, with a sad note in his voice, "but packing that thing in a twat is going to be like trying to stuff a wet noodle up a cat's ass."

"You asshole," said Feeb. "You asshole." He said it over and over.

When they took him into the emergency room at Chatham General, the nurse took one look, then leaned up against the wall and laughed for five minutes. When the doctor came in to see what was happening, she pointed at it with her finger. "Look at his weewee," she said. After which she and the doctor both leaned up against the wall and laughed for five minutes more.

Feeb stood there holding it in both hands, like it was a baby bird, saying, "Motherfuckermotherfuckermotherfucker." Until finally Jack and Whistler couldn't take it anymore either. They laughed so hard they fell down on the floor.

"It's ruined," said Feeb sadly.

When he was through laughing, the doctor wiped his eyes and blew his nose, then put Feeb up on the examination table to have a look at him. But there wasn't much he could do except reassure him that it would probably be all right.

"*Probably?*" said Feeb.

"Listen," said the doctor. "It may *look* a little funny. You never can tell. Maybe you'll be in demand. Women go for unusual things. Don't they, nurse?"

"Of course," she said. Then she leaned up against the wall again and laughed for another five minutes.

"Well," said the doctor, "let's have a look at it." And he reached out to touch it.

"Keep your hands to yourself," said Feeb.

Afterward, Jack and Whistler took him to Our House, a drive-in at the corner of Skidaway and Victory Drive that specialized in elaborate desserts, and bought him a hot fudge sundae with a sparkler in it.

"Feeling better?" Jack asked.

"Needs more fudge," said Feeb.

The team came out of the alumni game in pretty good shape, without any broken bones or sprains, and with their spirit topnotch. Feeb was the only one to complain, first claiming he had a charley horse, then a pulled muscle in his neck. But even he didn't carry on the way he usually did when a game was coming up. All in all, they seemed to be going into the season in just about the right frame of mind.

"As long as we don't peak too early and slide off for the game," said Chicken, who was a born worrier.

The schedule wasn't too bad—with the hardest teams coming on at the middle of the season. The first game was with Richmond Academy of Augusta, but the game would be played in Savannah, and it wasn't the toughest school on the schedule by a long shot.

The Cavaliers had finished third in the league the year before but had lost about half of their first team after graduation. Jimmy Dunn, the quarterback, and Danny Reese, the right half, were back from the 1946 team, along with Harper and Johnston, the ends, and Stude, a tackle. In addition, they also had a left halfback named David Quill, who would be starting for the first time. The sportswriters were all giving Quill the kind of thumb-in-the-dike treatment that they like to unload every now and then, whenever a good little man comes along, to remind everybody about the character-building aspects of the game. They were calling him "Little David" and "The Giant Killer" and things like that, with plenty of quotations from the Bible and Grantland Rice sprinkled in. Quill weighed 140 pounds—which wasn't all that small for a high school halfback in 1947. Whistler Whitfield weighed only 150.

But it was the beginning of the season, and they were looking for things to write about.

From Coach Garfield's point of view, the bad thing about Richmond Academy was that they were a passing team. He had wanted Boniface to go up against a running offense the first time out because of Jack.

"You can't have everything," he said.

Beginning on Wednesday, Jack started to point out

the importance of good, hard knocking at the very beginning of the game.

"We've got to play the whole four quarters," he said. "A good team won't fold up on you at the end anyway. But it won't hurt anything to set them on their cans right to start with." He looked at Feeb. "How much does the right tackle weigh?"

Feeb looked around at the rest of the players, then at Jack.

"Come on, Feeb. I know you looked it up."

"A hundred and ninety," he said.

"Program weight?"

"Yes," said Feeb. "That's what was in the newspapers."

"That means a hundred and eighty. Maybe a hundred and seventy-five. You'll have fifty pounds on him."

Feeb seesawed his hand back and forth. "Forty," he said.

"You've got to set him on his can the first time off the line."

Feeb rubbed his leg in an elaborate manner.

"How's your leg?"

"A little stiff," said Feeb. He rubbed his neck. "It's my neck really hurts."

Jack looked at him. "I don't want you to screw around, Feeb. I know you can't play the whole game. I'm asking you to hit your man the first time across."

Feeb made a whiny face.

"What was the score last year?"

Nobody said anything. At last Bo Hoerner spoke up. "They had a great team, man," he said.

"They finished third," said Jack.

"They had the team to make it," said Bo. "They lost second place on a tie."

"I know they beat you," said Jack. "And I know what the score was. I want one of you to say it out loud."

"Twenty-eight to six." Ducker said it, speaking very low.

"Okay," said Jack. "Remember those numbers. We're going to turn that around."

There was silence. "Dunn's a good quarterback," said Ducker. "He was throwing to Harper and Johnston last year too."

"Is he as good as Aaron?" said Jack.

Ducker looked at Aaron. "Shit no," he said.

"So we'll have to stop Dunn," said Jack.

Ducker thought a minute. "I fucking guess we will," he said.

"What'd he say?" said Frog.

"He said we'd have to stop Dunn," said Chicken. Then he turned to the players. "That goes double for me," he said.

Richmond Academy won the toss and elected to receive. Whistler got off a clean kick that Quill took inside his fifteen-yard line. He was fast all right, and he liked to jitterbug around a lot, but he didn't want anybody to get their hands on him, so he stepped out of bounds on purpose at the twenty-five-yard line, just in front of Flasher and Chippy Depeau.

Jack called a defensive huddle.

"He's going to pass," he said.

"How can you tell?" said Dimmy.

"That's what I would do," said Jack.

"Okay," said Ducker.

"Depeau," said Jack. Chippy Depeau played the middle of the line on the five-three defense. "You reach over and pull the center out as soon as he hikes the ball. Me and Hoy and Camack will shoot the hole. Feeb, you and Bo keep the guards from closing it up on us." He looked at Dimmy. "Are you listening, Camack?"

"What?" said Dimmy.

"We'll get Dunn," said Jack. "Just get through the hole and head for Dunn. Got that?"

"Head for Dunn," said Dimmy.

They spread out on the line, and the Richmond Academy center came up over the ball.

All three of them got through the hole, but Jack was the quickest, and he was the one that nailed him. Dunn was moving very gracefully and taking his time — like the whole thing was a foregone conclusion, or a drill of some kind. Jack caught up with him just as he turned around to deliver the ball, and he looked very surprised, then disappointed, when Jack dove in under his arm and cartwheeled him up in the air. He went straight up, did a slow turn end for end, with his arms and legs sticking out like the spokes of a wheel, then came down head first with a cracking sound on the fourteen-yard line. It was a hell of a jolt, but he managed to hang on to the ball. Jack reached down and gave him a hand to help him up.

"Fi-fi . . . fi-fi . . . fifty-five," he said, reading the number off Jack's jersey.

"Lynch," said Jack and patted him on the shoulder. "See you."

The Richmond team all looked at Jack sideways with their heads hanging down as they walked back to the huddle on the four-yard line. The longest look came from Quill, who was sucking his lips in and out and muttering under his breath.

"I don't think they took it serious," said Jack. "They're going to try it again." He looked at Chippy. "Pull him out of there again, Depeau," he said.

"How can you tell if it's a pass?" said Depeau.

"Start counting when they huddle," said Jack. "If you get to twenty before they break, it's going to be a pass."

"What if it ain't?" said Ducker.

"Watch Quill on a screen."

Dimmy squinted at the Richmond Academy huddle. "Quill," he said.

"Dunn," said Jack. "And, Hoy," he said, "you and Camack go in and take him. I'll stay back for the screen."

"Head for Dunn," said Dimmy, clapping his hands.

"Atta boy," said Jack. Then, "And, Hoy?"

"Yeah?"

"Try to give Quill a tap while you're in there. I don't think he really wants to play."

Camack caught Dunn by the jersey on the six-yard line and slammed him down on the ground like a bad poker hand. Ducker veered off so he could get at Quill, who was down in his blocking stance with his elbows up, looking like a photograph out of a book on how to play football. Ducker went into him like a freight train going into a tunnel, and he almost came out on the other side.

Both Quill and Dunn got up slowly. But they got up.

Jack looked at the down marker. "I'd get it out of there if it was me," he said. "Did the kicker play last year?"

"Who's the kicker?" said Ducker.

"Watch the center's head for a quick kick. If he puts it down, pull him out of there."

Ducker, Dimmy, and Jack all got into the backfield, but it was Frog who blocked the kick, taking one of his Nijinsky leaps that put his hand thirteen feet up in the air right in front of the ball. It hit him with a big splat that vibrated down his arm and shook some of the stuffing out of his helmet. But it wasn't as hard as one of Aaron's bullets, and he held onto it, coming down with it in the end zone.

"Is this the right end of the field?" he said, looking at Jack.

"Yes," said Jack.

"Then this is a touchdown?"

"That's what it is."

"I'll be goddamned," said Frog.

Whistler kicked the extra point, and Boniface led 7-0, with eleven minutes and nine seconds left to play in the quarter.

Nobody could believe it. Not from Richmond Academy or Boniface.

J. J. O'Brien was sitting on the Boniface bench, as usual, and when Frog scored the touchdown, he pulled out his checkbook and flashed off a check with the book braced on his knee.

"One hundred dollars to the man that brings me that ball," he said, waving the check over his head. "One hundred American dollars."

The whole Boniface bench looked at him for a minute, then all of them got up and galloped down under the scoreboard behind the goal to wait for Whistler's kick to come down so they could catch it. But the officials didn't like the way that looked, and they hustled them out, threatening to hold up the game until they all went back to the bench and sat down.

"That's all right, boys," said J. J. "The offer stands till the end of the game." Then he lit a cigar and stuck the check in his lapel pocket, hanging it out where everybody could see it.

"What if we lose?" somebody asked him.

J. J. looked up and down the faces on the bench. "Who said that?" he said. "What negative-minded, defeatist son of a bitch said that?" Nobody spoke. "I'm a man of my word, gentlemen," he said. "Win, lose, or draw, I'm paying for that football." He stuck the cigar back in his mouth and turned to watch the Boniface team coming down the field.

Boniface kicked off to Richmond again, then held for three downs. Whistler took the kick on his own thirty-five and ran it back to the fifty.

Somebody from Augusta must have thought that what was sauce for the goose would be sauce for the gander because on the first play from scrimmage their middle guard reached over and tried to pull Jack out of the line, the way Depeau had been doing to them. It was a bad move. Jack took him on his shoulder and drove him into both linebackers, who were trying to get in through the hole he was supposed to be making. It jammed the whole defensive center of their line. While that was happening, Dimmy went by with the ball, pushing the guard ahead of him to the forty-one-yard line.

Aaron called Dimmy up the middle four more times to the twenty-five. Then he gave Whistler the ball and sent him off the right side on a quick-opening play. There wasn't a Richmond Academy player standing at the line of scrimmage by the time Whistler got there, but he didn't get to see it because he was running with his eyes closed, a habit he'd developed the year before.

When he opened them, he was in the secondary, and Cowboy McGrath was putting his shoulder into Quill, just where the little man's jersey tucked into his pants. Quill's helmet was spinning up in the air like a big, white poker chip, and the only thing between Whistler and the goal line was Dunn—who played safety.

Whistler took off, making big, happy leaps. When he got to Dunn, he gave him his hip four times and took it away five, then shot by him on the right-hand side. Dunn just fell down flat on the football field and rolled over on his back with his arms reaching up into the air. When Whistler went over the goal line, he was practically walking. He stopped under the goalposts and jumped up and down a couple of times, then he touched the ball to the ground, very slow and dainty, with his leg pointing out behind him.

"Number two," he said.

By the end of the first quarter, Jack had collected a whole catalog of little moves and gestures that told him what Richmond Academy had in mind when they were on offense. He had his eye on Dunn to begin with, and right away he noticed that he would swing his head right and left when he was going to hand the ball off to one of his backs. On a pass, he would just get down behind the center and stare straight ahead. Quill was telegraphing, too, rocking his head back into his shoulder pads when the ball was coming to him. And Stude, the right tackle, made a limbering-up flourish with his elbow, getting into his stance when the run was coming his way. Jack passed the information on to the rest of the team and told them to keep their eyes out for other giveaway signs like that.

Boniface scored fourteen points a quarter until the last quarter, when they scored twenty. By then, four of Richmond Academy's first-string line were out of the game, as was Quill, and the coach was having to walk up and down the bench and hunt for the substitutes, who wouldn't answer when he called their names.

Whistler missed the last extra point and was so upset about it he sat down and started to cry.

Jack comforted him by patting him on the shoulder. "Look at the scoreboard, Whistler. You don't need to feel bad about it."

"Sixty-two to nothing." Bo Hoerner kept saying it over and over. "Jesus H. Christ! Sixty-two to nothing!"

"We took them by surprise," said Jack. "They thought they were playing us like last year."

"We beat the shit out of them is what we did," said Ducker. "Sheee — it!"

"We didn't do bad for the first game," said Jack. "We got nine more to go."

"Bring on the motherfuckers," said Feeb.

"Who?" said Dimmy.

Jack was too pessimistic. The Richmond Academy game was a preview of the season.

The second game was with Waycross. They played the game out of Savannah, and the score was 31-6. They should have beaten them more, only they were coming down off the high after stomping around on Richmond Academy so freely. Also the word had gone out on them, and Waycross was up for the game.

Then they played Valdosta in Savannah, beating them 7-0 with their defense. Valdosta was about to begin twenty years of winning seasons under Coach Wright Bazemore, but they hadn't quite gotten their feet planted yet. Bazemore was taking a professional attitude toward the game and had sent an assistant over to Waycross to scout them.

After Valdosta, there were three games on the road in the month of October — Decatur, which was just outside Atlanta, on the tenth, Columbus on the seventeenth, and Bibb High of Macon on the twenty-fourth. They won all three of them — 20-14, 38-6, and 14-13.

The scores made it look like Bibb had the best of the three teams, which they didn't. And Boniface ought to have beaten them worse than they did, only they were having to play against the officials that night. By the end of the game, Boniface had drawn over two hundred yards in penalties, with three touchdowns called back, and J. J. O'Brien was cooling his heels in the Bibb County jailhouse for breaking the head lineman's sternum with his cane.

The team was still steamed up about it the next week when Kose High came up to play them in Savannah. Before the first quarter was over, the first team had run up three touchdowns, and Chicken was afraid they were going to hurt themselves, so he pulled them out to let them cool off. Then he cleared the bench for the rest of the game, giving everybody on the squad enough playing time to get a letter out of it for the season.

The way Boniface was rushing around made the Kose team nervous at first. This was not because they were expecting to win, which they weren't, but because they were hoping not to get hurt. The Kose players had a kind of built-in long view of the game and were not inclined to get very personally involved, since their team had lost the last fifty-four games in a row. And as soon as the first team was taken out and the pace slowed down, they seemed to get about as much of a kick out of the touchdowns Boniface was scoring as the Boniface team itself did. Then the pace slowed down some more, and they began to get nervous again.

In the second half Cannady Teuton, the third-team quarterback, came in and started throwing a lot of incomplete passes, so that there were whole series of downs when the clock didn't seem to be moving at all. The more the game dragged on, the more nervous the Kose players got. They were counting on it being over by ten o'clock.

The only reason Kose had been able to field a football team in the first place was because the coach had emphasized the broadening aspects of the travel involved, with trips to places like Pembroke, and Darien, and Willie-by-the-Run to look forward to. As far as the sport of it was concerned, the boys on the team would just as soon have gone down to the Dorchester Swamp to hunt alligators and water moccasins. But most of them had never been more than five miles from home, so taking the trips was something else again. Just getting a Savannah game on the schedule had doubled the size of the squad. Also the coach had sweetened the deal with a personal promise that after the game he would take all of them down to the Shalimar Miniature Golf Course, then buy them a sundae with a sparkler in it at the Our House drive-in. The trip to Savannah was the high point of the season, and playing the game with Boniface was just the price they had to pay for it.

It was too high a price for the spectators who had come up with them to see the game. They all went out at the half and didn't come back. And the band sneaked off at the end of the third quarter.

All of this was tough on the players because the Shalimar was just down Victory Drive from the stadium, and every now and then they could hear the bass drum beating and a trumpet run coming in over the back of the stands. The cheerleaders hung on until the middle of the fourth quarter, when the Boniface quarterback threw three incomplete passes in a row. Then they got up and left, too, after giving a locomotive for the Alligators.

It was eleven-fifteen when the whistle blew ending the game, and all of the Kose players who weren't actually on the field were halfway out of the stadium when it did. The score was 85-0, but they couldn't have cared less. It was the hour they were worried about, not the score. All of them ran out of the stadium with their uniforms on, following the sound of the drum down Victory Drive, hoping they would get to the Shalimar before it closed.

For the Tattnall game, the team went up to Atlanta on the *Nancy Hanks*. During the ride, Jack could feel their spirits sinking, but he didn't know what was causing it, so he didn't know what to do about it. By the time the train pulled into the Central Station in Atlanta at one o'clock, the whole car was foggy with gloom.

Playing in Atlanta. That's what was doing it. The old Atlanta worm was into the apple, and the six-hour train ride gave them plenty of time to chew on it.

Jack tried to talk some backbone into them, but it didn't do any good, and Tattnall ran up a quick two-touchdown lead right away. They put only twelve points on the board because their kicker got the holder's hand on the first try, making him gun-shy, so that he dropped the pass from center on the second one.

Having played in New Orleans, where there was no Atlanta myth, Jack could see what a sorry team Tattnall really had. "They're shitty," he said. "I'm telling you — shitty."

But his teammates hadn't played in New Orleans, and they couldn't see it the way he did. Finally, the frustration took him out of himself, and, with two minutes to go in the first quarter, he did something that he had never done before. He took a swing at the Tattnall fullback when the fullback came up from the side and laid a block on him that carried him out of the play. The referee saw it and threw him out of the game.

The whole Boniface team stood watching him walk off the field like he was the last messenger out of the fort, and the Indians were closing in. Feeb starting to walk off with him, but Ducker grabbed him by the neck of his jersey and pulled him back. "We can do it without him," he said.

Everybody looked at him.

"Let's win it for Lynch," said Bo Hoerner.

"Kiss my ass, Hoerner," said Feeb.

"Let's win it for *us*," said Ducker.

Lulu and Ducker talked it up as much as they could, and they hustled enough to keep Tattnall from scoring again, but they couldn't get up the punch to put one over themselves.

Then, just before the half ended, Aaron sent Whistler off tackle to the right on a lucky call that caught the defense moving to the left. Whistler found himself in the clear and ran sixty-five yards for a touchdown just as the half ended. With the extra point, the score was 12-7.

Whistler came into the locker room at the half and threw his helmet against the wall. "They ain't worth a goddamn shit," he said.

"That's what I've been telling you," said Jack.

Whistler looked at him. "You're right," he said. "They ain't worth a goddamn shit." He looked around the locker room. "They ain't worth a goddamn *shit*," he said, raising his voice.

The second half they went out and scored forty-nine points, just to prove they could play with Lynch out of the game. It was the best two quarters they had all year.

The Brunswick game was easy, though not for Delmus Lamott. All deals were off, and he had to move around a lot more than he was accustomed to doing. Under the circumstances, James Farney couldn't plug all the holes for him—not with the other team really playing he couldn't. Well, not *all* the other team. Feeb worked out his agreement right off, then he kept trying to negotiate with Jack in the huddles, coming in with a new offer after every play. But finally Jack told him flat out to keep his mouth shut, and Feeb had to go back to Delmus with the sad news.

Delmus took it hard, but it depressed Feeb, too. "He's only a goddamn rich pussy," he said to Jack. "You got to be a fucking hard rock?"

It was an off night for Jack, but the team had found out they were able to go it without him, and they took up the slack, winning the game 28-0—though they should have won by twice that.

At the end of the first nine games, Boniface had a record that made it look like J. J.'s letter to the Pope had gotten through. The cheerleaders painted a big poster and put it on the trophy case in the front hall. It was green on a white background, with shamrocks in the corners, and it was a very impressive sight.

* * *

Sep. 19 — Richmond Academy — 62-0
Sep. 26 — Waycross — 31-6
Oct. 3 — Valdosta — 7-0
Oct. 10 — Decatur — 20-14
Oct. 17 — Columbus — 38-6
Oct. 24 — Bibb — 14-13
Oct. 31 — Kose — 85-0
Nov. 7 — Tattnall — 56-12
Nov. 14 — Glenn Academy — 28-0
Nov. 27 — COLD TURKEY FOR OGLETHORPE

The cheerleaders didn't put the statistics on the poster, but those were as impressive as the scores. Boniface had averaged 423 yards a game on offense — 239 yards passing (which was a new school record) and 184 yards rushing (which wasn't quite as good as the Horse Rooney team). It was the highest total offense in the history of the school.

But the season wasn't over yet.

In fact, looked at from a certain point of view, even with ninety percent of their games already played, the real season was still ahead of them. The alumni and J. J. were delirious about the way the team had done up to then, all right, but the glory of the whole season would be wiped out if they lost to the Big Blue of Oglethorpe in the Thanksgiving Day game. That was the one that counted.

On the Saturday afternoon before Thanksgiving,

Jack and Feeb had agreed to meet downtown and go to a movie. They were only doing light work at practice, and the extra time between games made them edgy. Besides, there was a Betty Grable musical on at the Lucas, and Feeb liked Betty Grable almost as much as he liked hot fudge sundaes. Jack went in early to shoot a couple of games of pool in Wooten's pool hall on Duke Street, to get up some money for the tickets.

Striper Wooten did a lot of bookmaking on athletic events and horse races, and most of the football players from Boniface spent some time there off and on, especially during the season, when Striper was particularly friendly. He liked to have them around then because he thought it was good for the betting, and he made them feel welcome, putting up autographed pictures of them behind the counter and letting them shoot a free game of pool now and then. Jack stroked a pretty good cue when he was feeling right, and that afternoon he took three in a row from Lulu Demarco, who was not a bad player himself. He won enough to pay their way into the show and to buy them a couple of beers afterward.

Wooten's was just at the corner of Reynolds Square, and the Lucas Theater was down the street at the corner of Abercorn. It was a warm day and the sun was out, so Jack went into the square to sit down on a bench and wait for Feeb. There was a little man in a gray suit, with a hat on, and Jack started up a park-bench conversation with him.

"Nice day," he said.

The man looked at him for a minute, then wet his lips with his tongue. "Little dry," he said.

"The rain comes earlier in the fall," said Jack.

"I like about seventy-five percent," said the man. "Humidity," he added. "I'm talking about humidity."

"I see," said Jack.

"Seventy or seventy-five," said the man. He wet his lips again as if he were tasting something. "About forty-five today," he said.

"You mean it makes you uncomfortable?" said Jack.

"No," said the man. "You can't get down for the low notes when you're too dried out."

Jack looked at him.

"Whistling," said the man. "I'm talking about whistling." He pursed his lips and gave a little trill.

"I see," said Jack. For a minute neither one of them said anything. "You live here?" said Jack.

"I'm staying at the Dobbs House," said the man. The Dobbs House was an old commercial hotel on the Bryan Street side of the square. "Just passing through."

"I see," said Jack. "You a salesman?"

"I'm retired," said the man. "Just moving around."

"Whistling around?" said Jack and laughed.

"Yes," said the man. He didn't laugh. "I was down in Florida last month. Orlando . . . St. Pete . . . Jacksonville . . . *too much* humidity in Florida. St. Augustine wasn't bad. About sixty. Only it's right on the beach. The wind dries you out."

"You mean you whistle for a living?"

"No," said the man. "I told you. I'm retired."

"You mean you do it for a hobby?" said Jack. "Something like that?"

The man looked at him. "I never thought of it as a hobby," he said. "Maybe you could call it that."

"And you travel *around* doing it?"

"Yes," said the man.

"You mean you don't do anything else?"

"My wife died four years ago. We lived in Akron, Ohio, but I never did like it. Too hot in the summer and cold in the winter." He stopped and wet his lips. "We lived there thirty-eight years. I couldn't stand the goddamned place."

"What about the humidity?" said Jack.

"Rotten," said the man. "Just rotten."

While they were talking, Feeb came up, and Jack told him about the man.

"You mean you do it for a living?" he said.

"No," said the man, "I'm retired."

"It's a hobby," said Jack.

"And you travel *around* to do it?" said Feeb.

"Some places are better than others. We went to Phoenix, Arizona, once. That was when my wife was still alive. Phoenix is the worst place I was ever in for whistling. You wouldn't *believe* the humidity in Phoenix." He shook his head.

"Could we hear you?" said Jack.

"Sure," said the man. "What would you like to hear?"

"How about 'Heartaches'?" said Jack. Elmo Tanner's record had been popular the winter before. It was the only whistling music Jack could think of.

The man nodded. "Tanner don't have the range I've got," he said. "It's a good tune, though." He ran his tongue over his lips to wet them. "It's a little dry today," he said.

He whistled "Heartaches" for them, but without the background music it didn't sound as good as Elmo Tanner.

"That's pretty good," said Jack.

"You mean you just travel around looking for places to *whistle*?" said Feeb. "That's *all* you do?"

"I'm retired," said the man.

"I know that," said Feeb, "but goddamn."

"I like to whistle," said the man.

Feeb looked at Jack, then back at the man. "That's crazy," he said.

"It sounded good," said Jack.

"It's not a good day for it," said the man. "The air's a little too dry."

"Well," said Jack. Feeb looked exasperated.

"I'm going up to Wilmington, North Carolina, tomorrow," said the man. "I figure it ought to be just about right this time of the year."

"Savannah's too dry?" said Jack.

"I thought it would be about right, but it's a little too far from the ocean," said the man. "Wilmington's not quite so far. And the river is bigger." He wet his lips. "I might try San Francisco if Wilmington don't work out."

"Come on," said Feeb. "It's time for the movie."

"Thank you for letting us hear you whistle," said Jack.

"That's all right," said the man. He did a rapid version of "Good Night, Ladies" with trills. It sounded as good as Elmo Tanner. "I do it for myself mostly, but I like to try it out on people now and then."

"Come *on*," said Feeb.

On the way to the theater, Feeb got more and more worked up about the man traveling around the country whistling.

"That's the craziest fucking thing I ever heard."

"He *likes* to do it," said Jack. "What difference does it make?"

"It's crazy, man. Crazy," said Feeb. "All he does is whistle. That's the craziest fucking thing I ever heard."

"I think it's pretty good, myself," said Jack. "He's doing what he likes to do."

# 5

Everything that happens in the world is taken personally by the people in Savannah — the way a tidal wave used to be taken by the natives in those old Jon Hall movies about the South seas. Only there is no volcano rumbling in the background, and no Maria Montez in a sarong to throw into it even if there were. Besides which, nobody, even in Savannah, is quite that pristine anymore. These days it's not something that hits you in the eye — nobody marches around with a severed head stuck on a pole, and virgins don't get thrown to the sharks. But, in spite of that, the circuits are still open between earthbound individuals and a cosmic infinity, and whatever happens, *anywhere*, is reduced to a local frame of reference in Savannah.

Whether or not that is a diminishment of the world, finally, is hard to say. It certainly tends to make life more important and interesting than it is when you start by admitting that nothing means anything, and whatever happens to you personally is of no special importance in the big scheme of things. Nobody in Savannah would admit to any such thing.

Father Dyer, the teacher of senior English at Boniface, tried once to get his class to agree with him that MacBeth's "sound and fury" speech at the end of the play was an accurate picture of the world in general.

"'Life is a tale told by an idiot,'" he said, shaking his head sadly. He was baiting them, mainly to make them talk about it. But he was also a glum man, who went around with his lower lip in his teeth, tuned in to the world's sad song.

"What does it matter?" he said.

"Excuse me, Father Dyer," said Feeb. Feeb liked to talk in class. "That's like getting the word from a guy with a tack in his foot. Look at the situation. It ain't exactly an Abbott and Costello routine we're talking about." Feeb ticked off MacBeth's troubles on his fingers. "He's been sweating all those people he croaked. His wife just killed herself. A bunch of trees is attacking his castle. MacDuff is going to kill shit out of him . . ." He didn't actually say shit, even though there were only boys in the class and Father Dyer had a high level of tolerance. What he said was "sh-t," swallowing the *i*. He looked around at the class, then back at Father Dyer. "What's he got to be happy about? That's Paul Muni stuff, man."

A good Savannah answer. Take everything personally, and don't try to push it out from there. The universe is something you don't fool around with. Even Feeb knew there were a good many people in the world who would go crazy if they had to sit in a booth at Theodore's eating hot fudge sundaes for the rest of their lives.

World War II was especially exciting for the people in Savannah because they all assumed that when the Germans invaded the United States they would set up the first beachhead down at Tybee Island. And children went to sleep at night dreaming about Japanese planes coming down the river from South Carolina to drop bombs on the Dixie Crystals Sugar Refinery and the Union Bag Paper Mill.

But the things that were really local drew the most attention, and, next to the St. Patrick's Day parade on Broughton Street, the Thanksgiving Day game between Boniface and Oglethorpe was the biggest local event of all.

The St. Patrick's Day parade got out of hand eventually, turning into a media event with lots of out-of-town people—mostly college students—drinking green beer and whiskey in the warm sunshine and getting sick on one another. In 1947 it was mostly a local affair, one for participants more than spectators, and there were some very strange things about it. Like the Shriner's Oriental Band had a very prominent place in it, as did the precision drill team from the Mickve Israel Synagogue on Gordon Street. Contemplating that situation could have turned up some interesting thoughts, but people in Savannah aren't very big on contemplation, so no one ever noticed anything strange about it; they just went ahead and enjoyed the parade. Because people in

Savannah *do* like parades very much. They like to look at parades, and they like to march in them. Parades are one of the things that people in Savannah like the best, because there is plenty of showiness to them, and they are loud, and they never last too long.

But the Thanksgiving Day game between Boniface and Oglethorpe was the *second* high point of the year.

The Chamber of Commerce people thought so well of it that they listed it in the "Annual Events" section of the brochure they put out to attract tourists, along with such other things as the Miss Savannah Beauty Contest, the Chatham Artillery anniversary, and the annual Interstate Sailboat Regatta at Wilmington Island. There were only eleven annual events listed altogether, one of which was the dog show, so by all local standards, even official ones, the game was very big indeed.

The two schools had been playing each other in interscholastic sports for a long time. The baseball series went back to 1894. But, in 1947, the football rivalry was only in its twenty-third year.

Up to 1925, the Boniface Fathers wouldn't let the boys field a team—though the Big Blue of Oglethorpe had been out there since 1919.

Knute Rockne had the George Gipp teams at Notre Dame in 1919 and 1920. Then Red Grange played at Illinois in 1923, and after that the whole country went football crazy—which was an outside influence that *did* work its way into Savannah. The Fathers resisted that pressure until the end of the 1924 season. But that was the year of the Four Horsemen, and, with the alumni practically beating down the doors, it got to be the next thing to a moral imperative that Boniface, being a Catholic school—a school in the image of Notre Dame, so to speak—should field a team. So the Fathers gave in in the summer of 1925.

It was so late in the year that getting Boniface a place on the Oglethorpe schedule wasn't an easy thing to do. But everybody could see that the game had to be played, so they finally settled on Thanksgiving Day—after Oglethorpe's regular season was over. It was a natural time for the game anyway, and once the series started they never bothered to change it.

Boniface must have been picking up inspiration out of South Bend because they won five of the six games they played that first season, then beat the Big Blue 30-10 in Grayson Stadium. J. J. O'Brien rushed out after the game and bought a turkey for every player on the squad.

The next year the signals weren't coming in too well, and Oglethorpe got even, wiping them up 43-6.

Over the whole series, Oglethorpe held the edge, having won fourteen of the twenty-two games, which was only natural, since they had ten times as many students as Boniface did—though half of them were girls.

But traditional rivalries are apt to turn up quirky games, and there was really no way to figure the odds on this one. You certainly couldn't predict the outcome on the basis of the season records in a given year. Some of the games that got the most hysterical advance notices turned out to be jaw-breaking bores once the teams got onto the field — shoving matches between the thirty-yard lines, with baseball scores, like 3-2 (1934) or 6-3 (1941), that put even the cheerleaders to sleep. The only team in memory that came up to its pregame press was the Horse Rooney team of 1942. For the rest of them, one man's guess was as good as the next. So the sportswriters had a field day, knowing that no one would hold them responsible for what they had said once the game was over.

Every year there was a very strong urge — which tended to become irresistible — to call it the "Battle of the Century." Oglethorpe hadn't done too well in 1947. They had gone 4-5-1, which, though it was the best year of the last three, was still not exactly grist for a legend mill. If they had called Boniface the "*Team* of the Century," that would have been accurate enough. But it was too close to an understatement to be considered.

There was only one publisher, but two newspapers, in Savannah. And the styles of the sports editors were a study in contrasts.

The *Evening News* had Westgate Finney, who was sixty-eight years old. He had a kind of archaic, patrician style, full of big words and alliteration, that he had picked up reading the old *Police Gazette* in his younger days. Westgate was a great, blimplike man — a combination of Richard Harding Davis and Major Hoople, with a swollen red face, crosshatched on the cheeks with purple, and a nose like an inflamed Bartlett pear. He was a man who could be defined by the accessories that he carried. He had a great number of them, but the ones he was most known for were his monocle, his calabash pipe, his lemon yellow spats, and his umbrella with the handle that folded out and turned it into a shooting stick. His way with words sent all the younger reporters up the walls five or six times a week, but he had an unassailable air of security and assurance about him and never seemed to notice the way they were carrying on.

It would have improved the way they felt about him if his copy hadn't always been the last to come in. All morning they would have to watch him working at it, his head down on his forearm, his nose almost touching the paper—like a man engraving Bible verses on the head of a pin—writing it out in longhand on a yellow legal pad with a big orange Parker fountain pen. His script averaged thirty-seven words to the line, and trying to get it into focus would have ruptured the eyes of a bald eagle. The stenographers who typed it out—who were only human—were always complaining about the damage it was doing to their eyeballs.

But Westgate remained above it all. For forty-nine years he had been the drinking crony of Garth McIlwain, the publisher—who was seventy-three and very feeble, but just far enough onto the near side of senility that his family couldn't sign him into an institution and take over the newspapers. Mr. McIlwain was thrilled to death with Westgate's style, and as long as he could hobble back and forth on his canes to board meetings, there wasn't any way, short of assassination, to get Westgate's column off the sports page.

The name of the column was "It Matters Not" — which was sort of an unfortunate name, unless you caught the Grantland Rice allusion and filled out the rest of the line. It never occurred to Westgate that anybody would miss it, and he hated being obvious above all things.

For all that the younger staff thought it was a scandal, the quaint lavender scent of the column did lend a certain air of distinction to the sports section and didn't do all that much damage — considering the average level of the rest of the writing in the paper. Especially in view of an editorial policy that gave up the front page to stories like: *AUTO CRASH CLAIMS SIX ON TYBEE ROAD* and *JONES STREET CONFECTIONARY ROBBED FOURTH TIME* — while putting items like the death of President Roosevelt and the attack on Pearl Harbor back in the Want-Ad pages.

On Sunday, November 23rd, Westgate's lead paragraph ran as follows:

### Giving Thanks

Our puissant Pilgrim progenitors little knew what cosmic clashes would be convened in consequence when first they sat down to table with their newfound friends of copper hue to break bread and requite their Lord and

Provider, and raise thanks unto Him for the bounteous harvest lavished upon them; marking the moment by laying knife and fork to the succulent flesh of *Melagris gallopavo* (the American turkey, as it is known along the Halls of Science). Nor could they possibly have peeled their ocular orbs to perceive precociously, far off, at the end of that continuous corridor of commemorative celebrations, the crowning culmination of God's cheerful bounteousness, in the imposing person of one JACK LYNCH. Center. Backer of Lines. And Mayhem Merchant *extraordinaire.* Number fifty-five of Boniface College. Had they, our fulgent Founding Fathers, been granted fateful foresight to see whereunto their Holiday would lead, its awesome apogee in this heroic, humble, Hibernian lad, they would have had greater cheer and gustatory gratification in that fulsome feast, toasting and retoasting the fivefold wisdom and will of perspicacious Providence, thus its wonders to perform. . . .

And so on, and on, for fourteen double-column inches. That one even brought the Linotype operator up to the editor-in-chief's office to complain. As usual, it didn't do any good at all. Mr. McIlwain thought it was wonderful.

Maybe Mr. McIlwain was right. Westgate's column was certainly the most distinctive one in the whole paper even though nobody else on the staff ever saw it that way. Spot Dillard was more to their taste — though not altogether so.

Spot Dillard was the sports editor on the *Morning Press*. He was thirty-one and had come up plagiarizing from more up-to-date writers, like Grantland Rice and

Bill Stern. A small, wall-eyed, squirrelly man, who looked as though they had pulled him off a south-bound Coastline freight train on his way to Florida, then dressed him in a double-breasted gray suit two sizes too large and stuck a gray felt hat on the back of his head. His costume never varied, and they speculated around the office whether or not he slept in his hat since no one had ever seen him without it. Myra Flounce, the copy editor, was mortally affronted when the men in the office got up a kitty which they offered to her if she would settle the question of whether or not he took off the hat when he made love. Everyone took it for granted that he slept in the suit.

Where Westgate Finney moved around the office with the ponderousness of a dirigible, Spot zigged and zagged like a balloon with the air coming out. Whatever he did was done in a fever, a cigarette hanging out of the corner of his mouth and his hat perched on the back of his head, like Hildy Johnson in *The Front Page*. His writing style was heavy on italics and exclamation points, and he banged everything out with his middle fingers on an old Underwood desk-model typewriter, his face screwed up and his head bent to one side so the smoke from his cigarette wouldn't collect under the brim of his hat and blind him. Now and then he would turn out a column in verse—when the fit was really on him. Those usually started out in a Grantland Rice vein, then fell off rapidly in the general direction of Edgar Guest—though Robert W. Service was Spot's favorite poet.

He wasn't any more up-to-date than Westgate was, really, but he got his copy in on time, and his other habits made him easier to live with, so everybody thought that he was.

The column he wrote was called *The SPOTlight*, and it always began: "Good morning, Mr. and Mrs. Sportsfan."

On the night of November 22nd — Saturday — he got falling down drunk on Pabst Blue Ribbon beer and homemade scuppernong wine — zigged into the city room and dashed off a thirty-two line poem — then zagged into the men's room, where he barfed up everything but the laces in his shoes and collapsed into the waste basket.

On the morning of November 23rd, his whole column was the poem, which was all they had to print.

### NUMBER FIFTY-FIVE

Out of the mists of Pestilence,
A Sterling hero came.
Destruction was his *Line-of-Work*,
*Jack Lynch* it was his name.

Oh! Kelly Green his jersey is,
His number, Fifty-five.
And when he glides onto the field,
His foes he eats alive!

He blocks and tackles everywhere,
He stops them great and small.
And rival teams must quake with fear,
When he hikes back the ball!

> Oh beautiful his body is!
> And graceful, more, his stride!
> He doesn't know the meaning of
> Such words as *Fear* and *Pride*!
>
> Jack Lynch, we do salute you!
> On this *Thanksgiving* Day.
> And we are thankful, *doubly*!
> That we can see you play.
>
> We know you'll give the best you have!
> When Thursday rolls around.
> And, win or lose, you'll play the *game*,
> Over the Gridiron ground.
>
> Then, when the game is over,
> The score writ on the wall,
> The Record hung behind you,
> You'll follow *Glory's* call.
>
> And into the mists of Pestilence,
> *You'll* go where Heroes came!
> Destruction was your *Line-of-Work*,
> *Jack Lynch* it was your name!

Mr. McIlwain didn't think it was as good as Westgate Finney's column was, but he thought it was better than average. It showed that Spot was girding up his loins to do justice to the upcoming battle of the century.

Spot himself didn't remember having written it, and he spent most of Sunday night trying to get somebody else to confess to having done it. They kept telling him that he had done it himself, but he didn't believe them. "Come on, now," he said. "Which one of you assholes wrote that piece of crap?"

※ ※ ※

"Have you seen him? Have you seen the motherfucker?" It was Monday morning, and Feeb was blocking the door to Father Dyer's homeroom, each hand on a jamb, and his head sawing from side to side.

"What're you talking about Feeb?" said Jack. It never occurred to him that Feeb would be upset about anything connected with football.

"Ducker," said Feeb. "Have you seen Ducker?"

Jack looked at him. "No," he said.

"The motherfucker," said Feeb. "The fucking motherfucker."

"Well?" said Jack. He waited. "What about Ducker?"

"He broke his leg."

Jack looked at him without saying anything, just pulling his eyebrows together a little.

"Him and Whitfield and Camack," said Feeb. "The motherfuckers went for the coffin."

"Hoy and Whitfield *and* Camack all broke their leg?"

"Ducker broke his leg," said Feeb. "All of them went for the coffin."

In a traditional rivalry like the one between Boniface and Oglethorpe, one that keeps up year after year, a lot of little traditions tend to accumulate around the big one as time goes by. That way more people can get in on it and feel like they're taking part in the main tradition, even when they can't do it directly.

The big secondary tradition of the Boniface-Oglethorpe game was burning the coffin.

During the week before Thanksgiving week, a small, select group of students at each school would go into hiding and build a big dummy coffin out of wood, which they would paint in the colors of the other school, with the name lettered on the side and crepe paper tassels and flowers all over it. On Monday of Thanksgiving week, each school would set up the coffin it had built on sawhorses in front of its main entrance and post a guard to protect it. After the game, on Thursday night, the winner would take the loser's coffin out to Forsythe Park and make a bonfire and burn it in a victory celebration.

Part of the tradition was that once the coffin got set up under guard in front of the school, it had to be left alone. But during the week when it was being built, stealing it was the name of the game, if anybody could get onto where the hidden workshop was. A kind of guerrilla war developed, with hunting parties out every night cruising around town trying to find the opponent's secret location.

The spirit of the search wasn't all that frivolous and innocent, and there was nothing in the tradition about the fights being barehanded. No fatalities ever resulted, but whenever the scouts ran into each other, there was likely to be an assortment of broken bones and a certain amount of blood on the ground afterwards. That was a measure of how much was at stake. Bringing back the coffin was very big for status, being just a notch below playing in the game itself.

Losing your coffin was also very important. It could even affect the outcome of the game.

Because of the mayhem involved in the raids, both coaches had strict rules that football players could not take part in the search because they needed to be kept whole for the game itself. Ducker, Whistler, and Dimmy had broken the rule.

Whistler was the one who had found out where Oglethorpe was building the Boniface coffin. Which was no Sam Spade operation, since it was in Hoke Smith's garage and Hoke lived right next door to him. Whistler watched them out the window until he couldn't stand it any longer. Then he passed the word to Ducker. Dimmy got in on it because his father had a pickup truck and they could carry the coffin off in it.

The idea—it was Whistler's, and he had gotten it from watching Errol Flynn commando movies during the war—was that a small group of them could make a quick raid in the middle of the night and get away before anybody knew what had happened.

"They'll never know," he said, "what fucking hit them."

The plan went just the way it was supposed to—up to a point. There were two Oglethorpe boys standing guard in the garage, but Ducker didn't even have to threaten them to back them off.

The trouble was Dimmy. They had the coffin in the truck, with Dimmy at the wheel, and Whistler and Ducker in the back holding on to it, since it was too long to go in with the tailgate up. The truck was parked in the alley behind Hoke's house, a tight place to negotiate and one that needed attention, which was the chief thing Dimmy couldn't give to it—or to anything else, for that matter. He slammed into low gear, raced the engine, and let out the clutch, lurching the pickup in short, rocking hops that dumped Ducker into the alley on his head and shot the coffin out over the tailgate. When he banged into the garage across the way, Dimmy shoved the gear shift up into reverse and ricocheted backward over Ducker's leg. Whistler yelled at him through the window of the cab, but Dimmy was focusing his attention on the driving and he didn't hear him. He put the truck back into first and went over Ducker again going forward.

Whistler finally got into the cab and jerked the key out of the ignition, but by the time he did, Dimmy was going over Ducker for the fourth time, the right wheel working down his leg with each pass, from just below his knee to his foot. The alley was sandy and loose, and Ducker's leg was such a piece of meat that the first three passes hurt the truck more than they did him. But the fourth pass was over his ankle, and that time something snapped.

After the doctors fixed him up, there was some serious doubt whether Ducker would ever walk right again. But that was a long-range problem and was Ducker's personal lookout. The immediate concern, which had more people involved in it, was that he wouldn't be able to play in the game.

"Why'd you do it, Hoy?" Jack looked down at the big white club of plaster of Paris, with Ducker's toes sticking out the hole at the end. Dimmy had already written his name on the cast. Once across the instep, and once, longways, up the side.

Ducker didn't want to talk about it. "Shit, Lynch," he said.

"We *had* to do it, man," said Whistler. "They was right out my bedroom window. I was watching them all week."

"You could have told somebody else and let them do it. Why'd you have to go after it yourself?"

"It was right out the *window*, man," said Whistler. "There wasn't nothing to it."

Jack looked down at Ducker's cast, then back at Whistler. "I can see there wasn't."

"We got the fucking coffin," said Whistler. "It was Dimmy backing up the truck broke Hoy's leg."

"I can still get around pretty good," said Ducker. He held the crutches in one hand and hobbled back and forth on the cast to show them.

"No shit," said Jack.

"Fuck it," said Ducker. He put the crutches back under his arms and went swinging away down the hall.

"We got the fucking coffin," said Whistler. Then he went away down the hall after Ducker.

"What're we going to do, Jack?" said Feeb. "What're we fucking going to do without Ducker?"

"You sound like we had a choice," said Jack. Then he added, "It's not the end of the world, Feeb. We've been lucky nobody got hurt up to now." He thought about it for a while, then shook his head. "Maybe it's the end of the world," he said.

While they were talking, Dimmy came up. "Did you see the coffin?" he said. "Me and Whitfield and Hoy got Oglethorpe's coffin Saturday night."

"We heard," said Feeb.

"Hey," said Dimmy. "How about that?" He sounded pleased about getting the coffin. "It's kind of busted up, but we got it."

"Hard on Hoy," said Feeb.

"Yeah," said Dimmy. "He hurt his foot."

"I hear you were driving," said Feeb.

"My old man won't let nobody else touch his truck."

Jack turned and started away.

"It's got this clutch . . . ," said Dimmy.

"Fuck off, Camack," said Feeb.

Dimmy stood in front of him, hunched over, his brows pulling down. His face clouded. "What'd you say?"

"I said you blew the fucking game," said Feeb.

"Oh," said Dimmy. He stood there, thinking about it, his eyes moving from side to side under the bony ledge of his brow, an expression on his face like a chimpanzee trying to decide between a coconut and a banana. For a minute and a half he didn't say anything.

"What game?" he said at last.

Coach Garfield didn't know what to do about it.

"I don't know what to do about it," he said, twirling his whistle on its chain, wrapping it around his finger. He had gotten Jack out of his English class to talk to him. "I swear to God," he said, "I don't know what to do about it."

"Demarco's got the best spirit," said Jack.

Chicken looked at him, then twirled the whistle the other way. "Demarco's too light to play tackle. What do you think?"

"Demarco can play center," said Jack. "I'll play tackle."

"Demarco can't play center," said Chicken.

"He played against Tattnall and Kose."

Chicken looked at him. "*Everybody* played against Kose."

"He played against Tattnall."

Chicken twirled the whistle again. "Demarco's too little."

Jack watched him unwind the whistle, then wind it up the other way. "If I wasn't here, who would be playing center?"

"It wouldn't be Demarco," said Chicken. "He would have something broke by now."

"Who would you have *started* at center?"

"That was in the *old* days," said Chicken. "I *got* a

center. What I need is a tackle."

"We're lucky nobody's been hurt up to now," said Jack. "Lulu's the best man you've got for spirit."

"What about Sullivan?" said Chicken. "He's a hundred and eighty."

"You're making too much of size. Sullivan won't come on with the team the way Demarco will. Not this year. Next year he'll be fine."

"You think Demarco can move them out?"

"He moved them out pretty good in the Tattnall game. He won't let them *in*. If we can get him to submarine, he might move them out."

"I wish he had forty more pounds on him."

"I wish he had a *hundred* more pounds on him. We got three days, Coach."

"I just don't know," said Chicken, twirling his whistle. "I just don't know."

So they moved Lulu in at center on offense, with Jack playing tackle. On defense, Jack went back to his old linebacker's position.

"I want your head in this game too, Lulu," said Jack. "You pay attention. If you get something busted, we're really up the creek."

"I'll try," said Lulu.

"I know you'll try. I want you to be *careful*."

There wasn't any point in trying to keep Ducker's leg a secret from the Oglethorpe team, not with Dimmy going around talking about it and lining up people to autograph the cast. The way Dimmy looked at it, Boniface hadn't gotten Oglethorpe's coffin since 1942, but they played the game every year.

Actually, the Oglethorpe team didn't need all the psychological advantage they were getting out of Ducker's leg.

They were a big team — ten pounds heavier than Boniface from end to end — though they didn't have any real stars to focus their game. The traveling squad had forty-nine men on it, and the first two teams had averaged just over two quarters' playing time per game, with a third-team average of eight quarters' playing time for the season. They couldn't get eleven men on the field all at once as good as the eleven men Boniface had, but there were thirty-five or so who were only a notch below that level, and they could run them in and out all day long. Depth was the thing that a team needed to play them. Which was the one thing Boniface didn't have. Even before Ducker broke his leg.

"We'll have to get us twenty-one points in the first half to beat them," said Chicken. He and Jack had talked over the strategy for the game beforehand, but Chicken was the one who told the team about it.

"Their home-game squad is nearabout twice the size of ours," he said. "And they've got the biggest third-team line in the state."

"Only they can't put but eleven of them out there at a time," said Jack.

Chicken looked at him. "Eleven at a time," he said.

\* \* \*

It wasn't just the size of the squad that hurt. It was also the way they played the game. Oglethorpe was one of those teams that couldn't seem to score many touchdowns, but they would beat you to death on the field trying. That was because Faro Wicker, their coach, knew all there was to know about conditioning but didn't know the first thing about strategy. "Lacy-drawer stuff" is what he called it.

Faro had played end on a running team at the University of Georgia in the early thirties, which had given him a very physical conception of the game. He was in his fourteenth year as head coach at Oglethorpe, and in the fourteen years he had had one undefeated team — in 1938 — and nine winning seasons. Considering the material he had, that wasn't a very impressive record. Oglethorpe had always had the biggest enrollment of any high school in the state, and Faro could have dressed out a hundred players a year if he could have found somebody to put up the money for the uniforms.

Faro was big and rawboned, and his years in the city had not rubbed the cracker off him. He still walked like he was hopping furrows, and he carried his elbows in tight to his sides, with his forearms winged out. Eighteen years after he left the ten-acre farm he was raised on in Woad, Georgia, you could have backed a plow up to him and the handles would have slipped right into his hands.

Faro's approach to football was strong on basics, but

there wasn't any long view about it at all. Every year he would get a herd of big boys onto the team—*herd* was Faro's term, and it expressed just about the degree of sentiment he felt for them—then give them plenty of punishment during the practice sessions to harden them up and make them mean. The way he saw it, his job started on Monday afternoon and ended after practice on Friday. Friday night was in God's hands. He was interested in the way it turned out, of course, but he didn't feel like there was anything he could do about it.

So Oglethorpe lost a lot. But they lost in a way that was extremely hard on the team that beat them. The Oglethorpe players never seemed to get their minds more than five yards off the line of scrimmage. By the time they went away and left you alone, you would be hurting too much to notice how many points there were on the scoreboard anyway. It was shortsighted football, but it was pure bloody murder while the game lasted.

"We'll have to throw a lot of short passes and hit for quick ones into the line," said Jack. "We'll let you drop a bomb on them now and then, Aaron. But don't count on doing it all afternoon. The less time we have to spend pushing them around on the line, the better. We'd have to take too much punishment." He looked at Aaron. "Are you listening?"

"Quick stuff," said Aaron.

"Same thing for wide runs." He turned to Dimmy. "You're the one will have to carry us, Camack. You and Frog."

Frog ate his bubble. "What'd he say?" he said.

Losing Ducker didn't change the game plan that much, but it meant that all of them were going to have to take more punishment than they had planned on.

# 6

Thanksgiving Day was clear and cold—forty-two degrees, and no wind blowing. After an extra week of rest, the field was tight and hard.

When the teams came out for the pregame warmup, there were six rows of ten men each on the Oglethorpe end of the field, with three captains to call out numbers for the exercises. It was pretty much the same story year after year, except that this year the Boniface team was thinking about winning. Still, the fans weren't especially downhearted because of it.

J. J. O'Brien had broken out his World War I uniform for the occasion, ribbons and all. The last time he had done that was for the 1942 game, which Boniface had won, and he was out to work the charm again. Also he had pushed up the offer for the game ball to $150, though he didn't say anything about "win, lose, or draw." He had the money in silver dollars, and before the game he set it up on a card table in the locker room—fifteen stacks of ten—so they could all see what it looked like.

"No paper, boys," he said. "Silver." He held up one

of the silver dollars between his thumb and forefinger. "Pure coin of the realm," he said.

After he was sure everybody had seen them, J. J. put the coins into the pockets of his cartridge belt, which he wore during the game.

When they went out for the toss of the coin, the whole Boniface first team walked to the center of the field. All of them were seniors, and they had decided that they would have eleven co-captains for their last game at Boniface. Oglethorpe had three. It was the only time the Big Blue would be outnumbered that day.

Oglethorpe won the toss and elected to receive. Bammer Kicklighter took Whistler's kickoff on the five-yard line and ran it back to the twenty, where Lulu and Flasher brought him down. Oglethorpe ran two end sweeps for seven yards, then sent their fullback up the middle for no gain. Whistler took the punt on his own thirty-five and ran it back to the fifty.

Aaron threw two spot passes to Frog for a first down at the Oglethorpe thirty-eight, then gave it to Dimmy nine times in a row up the middle to the two. The tenth time he faked to Dimmy and gave the ball to Whistler, who went wide around end and walked into the end zone with the nearest Oglethorpe player fifteen yards away.

The kick was good, and Boniface led 7-0 with six minutes to go in the quarter.

"Nothing fucking to it," said Whistler as they went back downfield.

The line play had been crisp on the drive, but the Boniface team was holding up well, and even Feeb was taking out his man. "Bring on the motherfuckers," he said.

On their second series, Oglethorpe made two first downs, getting the ball out to the fifty. Then the quarterback fumbled, and Lulu recovered for Boniface on the forty-five. Jack worried about Lulu being on the bottom of the pile, but they untangled and he walked back to the huddle all right.

"You okay?" he asked.

"We're going to fucking take them, man," said Lulu.

Aaron threw two short passes to Frog for a first down on the Oglethorpe thirty-two. Then the whistle blew ending the quarter, and the Oglethorpe second team came in. Their clean uniforms were crisp and sharp-looking.

Dimmy ran three times for nine yards, making it fourth and one on the twenty-three. There were ten minutes and thirteen seconds left to play in the half.

"We shouldn't go for it outside the twenty," said Jack. "Whistler can lay it out inside the five."

"We got fourteen points to go," said Whistler.

Jack looked at him.

"Twenty-one points at the half. You said it, Lynch."

"Can you hold them off for a long one?" said Aaron.

Jack looked at him. "I don't like to go for the chancy stuff when we're ahead," he said.

"We got two more to go," said Whistler.

"All the way, Flasher," said Aaron.

Jack didn't say anything, and Lulu broke the huddle. Digger Spode, who was playing middle guard over Lulu, got by him, and almost brought Aaron down. But Flasher was in under the goalposts before anybody missed him. The ball dropped into his hands, and he held on for another six points.

Whistler kicked the extra point, and Boniface led 14-0.

On the first play from scrimmage after the kickoff, Lulu got up limping from the pile.

"It ain't nothing," he said.

But Jack sent him to the sidelines, with instructions to have Sullivan come in as a replacement.

J. J. came up to Lulu and asked how he was feeling. "You're playing a fine game, lad," he said. "They need you out there."

Lulu tried to run sprints up and down the sidelines, but it was clear that his ankle was hurting him.

J. J. looked at Dr. Vespers, the team physician. "Take him under the stands and fix him up." Dr. Vespers looked at J. J., then got his bag and took Lulu under the bleachers to examine him. He went over the ankle carefully to be sure that it wasn't broken, then gave him a shot of Novocaine.

While Lulu was out, Oglethorpe ran seven plays to the forty. Then Whistler intercepted a pass, and Boniface had it first and ten at their own forty-five. On the exchange of the ball, the Oglethorpe third team came in, and their uniforms looked even cleaner and crisper than the second team's had.

"There's a million of the fuckers," said Whistler.

On the first down, Aaron threw a short pass to Frog. Frog caught it on the Oglethorpe forty-eight, but the cornerback came up fast and gave him a good, sharp rap, which turned him around and started him off toward the Boniface goal line. The team was slow reacting, and he was down to the five-yard line before Flasher caught up with him and brought him down.

"Kick it out, Whitfield," said Jack.

Oglethorpe's first team came in to attempt to block the punt, and Jack moved over to center the ball. The Oglethorpe left tackle grabbed Lulu by the jersey and yanked him out of the line, then got into the backfield and blocked Whistler's punt. The Oglethorpe end fell on it in the end zone, and they were on the board with their first six points. The kick was good, and with four minutes and twenty-three seconds left to play in the half the score was 14-7.

After the kickoff, the Boniface drive stalled with fourth and four to go on the thirty-eight. Then Bammer Kicklighter got away from Flasher on the punt return, cut for the sidelines, and almost outran the team. Aaron bumped him out on the Boniface forty-three. Oglethorpe ran three plays for a first down on the thirty-two. Then Boniface held them for three yards on the next three.

With fourth and seven for Oglethorpe on the Boniface twenty-nine and forty-five seconds left to play in the half, a substitute came out from the bench. There had been so many, nobody on the Boniface team paid any attention to him. Then, when they came out of the huddle, they lined up in place-kicking formation.

Jack looked at the kicker—who was wearing number 99. "When did they get a kicker?" he said. Oglethorpe's kicking game had been awful for the last three seasons, but somewhere during the last two weeks Faro had found himself a leg. It was something Jack hadn't counted on.

"Get up there and block it, Frog," he said. "He won't get it in there from here."

Frog's reflexes were slowing down, and the ball sailed off just over his fingertips, coming down in the end zone bleachers. The referee threw up his hands, and, with thirty-eight seconds left to play in the half, the score was 14-10.

"Where'd he come from?" said Jack. "Ninety-nine's not even on the program."

"How the shit would I know?" said Whistler. "They probably got eight more teams we never fucking heard of."

"I hadn't counted on a kicker," said Jack. "We're going to have to hold them outside the thirty."

Nobody said anything for a minute.

"Jesus God," said Whistler.

Going off the field at the half, Jack noticed the way Lulu was walking. "What'd they do to you, Lulu? You all right?"

"Yeah," said Lulu. "I don't feel nothin'. They fixed me up good."

Jack looked down at the way he was walking. "Did Vespers give you a needle?"

Lulu looked at him. "Like I said. He fixed me up. Don't worry about it."

In the locker room, Jack complained to Dr. Vespers. "Getting hurt is the only thing that keeps him from getting killed," he said.

J. J. O'Brien heard him talking and came over and put his arm around Jack's shoulder. "Don't argue with the doctor," he said. "The lad's fine." He looked at Lulu. "How do you feel, young man?"

"I'm okay," said Lulu. "My leg's okay."

"Don't worry, Jack," said J. J. "The doctor always knows best."

Chicken came into the locker room twirling his whistle. "Where'd the kicker come from? Oglethorpe don't have no kicker."

"They got one now," said Whistler. "Forty-five fucking yards."

"We're going to have to keep them outside the thirty," said Jack. "I hadn't counted on a kicker."

Nobody said anything.

"My ass is dragging, man," said Feeb.

"Your ass is *always* dragging, man," said Whistler.

"We got a better team," said Jack.

Feeb dropped his helmet on the floor and leaned back against the lockers. "*Dragging*, man," he said.

"Let's win this one for Ducker," said Bo Hoerner.

"That asshole?" said Feeb.

The truth was they were missing Ducker sorely. Lulu had the spirit, but he couldn't power into the backfield to jam up plays the way Ducker could do it. Just hearing his name made them sad and resentful, reminding them how tired they were.

"Feeling under the weather, boys?" J. J. had climbed up onto a bench where everybody could see him. "A little fatigued and dejected?" He held up a small bottle of tablets. "Here's just what the doctor ordered," he said. "Chase your blues away."

They looked up at the bottle. Chicken twirled his whistle, but he didn't say anything.

"What you got there, Mr. O'Brien?" said Whistler.

"Energy," said J. J. "En-ur-gee." He opened the bottle and took out one of the tablets, holding it up where they could see it. It was smaller than an aspirin and pale yellow. "One of these little beauties, and you'll have your second wind in no time, boys." He sounded as if he was going to try to sell them.

"Hurry-up stuff," said Jack.

Chicken looked at Jack, then nodded his head. "I think not," he said. "Thanks just the same."

J. J. frowned. "Dr. Vespers wouldn't give you anything that would harm you young men. This is pure medicinal Dexadrine." He put the emphasis on *pure*, saying "pee-yore." "I've got a signed prescription for every man on this team. This is absolutely legal."

"You don't take that stuff in the middle of a game," said Jack. He looked at Coach Garfield. "Some people go crazy on it. You should have brought it around last week."

"You think Dr. Vespers would give you anything to hurt you?" said J. J. and began passing out the tablets. Jack looked at Chicken.

"It's illegal," said Chicken. "Jack's right. You're not going to take any of that stuff."

J. J. looked at him. "Dexadrine is *not* illegal," he said. "We got a licensed physician to sign the prescriptions."

"*Taking* them is illegal," said Chicken. "Thank you, Mr. O'Brien. I know you're thinking of the team. But I wouldn't want anybody to get in trouble."

J. J. looked at him, then held out the bottle. "Put them back, boys," he said. "You've got to listen to your coach."

"Much obliged, Mr. O'Brien," said Chicken. He was looking down at the floor. "I wouldn't want anybody to get in trouble."

"Well," said J. J. O'Brien. He picked up a glass of water and shook three pills out of one of the vials. "I paid for it. I hate to see it go to waste." He threw back his head and popped them into his mouth, then took a drink of water. "Put them in the valise, Dr. Vespers," he said, handing the vial to the doctor. He didn't look at anyone but walked out of the room looking straight ahead. "We'll be standing by," he said. "In case you need us."

"My ass is dragging, man," said Whistler.

"That's Feeb's line," said Jack. He looked at the two of them. "I want you both to get it up."

"I could have used some of that stuff, man," said Whistler. "My ass is *dragging*!"

Jack didn't look at him. He looked at Lulu. "Dr. Vespers gave Lulu a shot of Novocaine." He looked at Lulu's leg. "He ought not be playing on that foot when he can't feel it."

Chicken looked at Lulu. "Come here, Demarco," he said.

"I'm okay, Coach," he said.

"Did Dr. Vespers put Novocaine in your leg?"

"Maybe just a little. It feels okay, Coach. I could tell if something was wrong."

"Come here," said Chicken.

Lulu got up, trying to walk naturally.

"You're out of the game, Demarco," said Chicken. "You could hurt yourself bad."

"I'm okay, Coach," he said. "I'm *okay*."

Chicken wasn't paying any attention to him. "You go back to center, Lynch," he said. "Sullivan. You'll go in at tackle."

"Coach . . . ," said Lulu.

Chicken turned to him. "I hate to be the one to say this, Demarco, but it's only a goddamn *game*. You stay here and get your leg taped up. You shouldn't even be walking on it."

"Get Dr. Vespers," said Lulu. "See what Dr. Vespers thinks about it."

Chicken looked at his watch. He seemed surprised. "Time to go," he said. "You got to hang in there for twenty-four more minutes."

"Yeabo," said Bo Hoerner.

"Jesus Christ," said Feeb.

On the way out of the dressing room, they passed Dr. Vespers and J. J. O'Brien. J. J. was climbing up the drain pipe and had gotten about halfway up the side of the building. Dr. Vespers was pleading with him to come down. "It works faster with some people than others," he said. Then he added, "Call the fire department. I want a net here when he passes out."

Boniface took the kickoff and got it back to the Oglethorpe thirty-eight, then ran out of gas and had to punt. Kicklighter took the ball on his own ten and ran it out to the twenty-five. They worked it up the field in short, steady bursts, three and four yards at a time, to the Boniface twenty-six. Then Kicklighter fumbled and recovered on the twenty-five. It was fourth and three, so number 99 came in and kicked another field goal, making the score 14-13. The Boniface team was visibly sagging. They didn't seem to have any punch at all.

Whistler took the kickoff on his own fifteen, and four Oglethorpe players nailed him before he could take a step. Then Dimmy got four yards on three carries, and they had to punt the ball away.

In two series of downs, Oglethorpe was back down inside the Boniface twenty-five. Somehow Jack got them to stiffen and hold for three downs. So it was fourth and six, and number 99 came in to kick the field goal that would put them in front.

Jack called a time-out to try to talk some backbone into them. "Get up, Feeb," said Jack. Feeb was sitting down, which was strictly against the rules. They weren't even supposed to go down on a knee when they were on the field.

"Fuck it," said Feeb.

"Get up, or I'll kick you up," said Jack. Feeb looked at him, gave him a Boy Scout salute, then waved it into a finger. He got up, but he got up slowly.

"We're all fucking beat, Lynch," said Whistler. "Look at that bench over there," he nodded his head to the Oglethorpe side.

"I played against four different men already," said Feeb. "How many more of the motherfuckers you think I've got to go?"

Jack looked around at them. "This is the last game you're ever going to play for Boniface," he said.

"Is that a motherfucking promise?" said Feeb.

"You going to throw it away?"

"Man," said Whistler, "I'm fucking tired." He looked across to where the Oglethorpe team was huddling. "As soon as that little pissant puts it up there, we're going to be two points behind."

The referee blew the whistle, and they lined up for the play. Jack looked over the line at number 99, who was swinging his leg in little practice kicks, waiting for the ball to be snapped.

Number 99 was small and skinny, with two big yellow teeth poking out of his mouth, one lapping over the other, and no chin at all. He kept sucking on his teeth, sliding his upper lip down and back, so the teeth looked like they were popping in and out of his mouth. Nothing he had on fitted him. His jersey was too big, and his helmet was too small. It was a costume, not a uniform. He didn't look like a football player at all.

Jack was not inclined to hate a face, but he couldn't keep his eyes off number 99.

Before Digger Spode went down over the ball, he looked up at Jack and shot him a face full of teeth. "Watch your ass, Lynch," he said. He held up three fingers. "Big three coming up."

When the ball was snapped, Jack was over Digger and into the backfield like a shot. The Oglethorpe quarterback heard the cracking sound, and the ball sailed by him sitting there, his hands stretched out to catch it, but watching Jack instead. Number 99 froze, a terrified look on his face, his teeth sticking out bigger than ever. Jack put an elbow into him going by after the ball. He picked it up on the forty-one, then started for the goal without looking back. Bammer caught up with him on the

Oglethorpe thirty-two and rode his shoulders to the twenty-two, where three other Oglethorpe players caught up with them and brought them down.

Bo Hoerner was beside himself. He slapped Jack on the back. "Great, man. Great!" he said.

"Let's get it over," said Jack. They huddled with more spirit than they'd had since the first quarter, and Dimmy in particular seemed to be feeling pepped up.

While Aaron was calling signals, Dimmy stepped back out of the huddle and ran around it twice on the outside in a funny, dancing kind of step, making a rap-bap-bap noise, like a child imitating a machine gun. Then he stepped back into his place and clapped his hands together. "Gimmie da goddamn ball," he said.

They couldn't get his attention to run anything else, so Aaron called him up the middle. While Jack was taking out his man, Dimmy went by him like a freight train, picking up Digger on his shoulder and running off with him to the nine-yard line.

When they huddled again, Dimmy didn't come into the huddle at all. He spent the whole time running around on the outside in a prancing, high-kneed step, saying, "We got the *coff*-in. We got the *coff*-in." Over and over.

"What's got into Camack?" said Jack.

Whistler giggled, then reached across the huddle and tapped Jack on the helmet. "We took the fucking prescription, man," he said. Then he stood up and flexed his biceps like a picture in a Charles Atlas advertisement.

"Feel that arm," he said. Then he stepped out of the huddle and high-stepped around with Dimmy a couple of times.

Aaron ran Dimmy up the middle again, there being nothing else he could do. Dimmy went into the end zone dragging three men behind him and pushing two in front. He was humming the Boniface fight song all the way.

"Six points," he said, coming back to the huddle. "Six big points and the *coff*-in, *coff*-in . . . rooty-tooty-tooty . . . bap-bap-bap . . ."

"We better run it over," said Jack. "I wouldn't trust Whistler's kicking just now."

So they gave it to Dimmy again, and he took it in for the twenty-first point.

"How many of you took the pill?" said Jack when they huddled for the kickoff. Nobody said anything, but Feeb giggled and tried to give Jack a frog on the arm.

"Finnechairo?" said Jack. Frog was the one he was most worried about.

"Huh?" said Frog. He blew a bubble.

"Stick with your Fleer's, Frog," he said.

"What'd he say?" said Frog, trying to lift the flap of his helmet.

Dimmy was the hardest to control. Whistler calmed down pretty well after the first high passed off and was no harder to deal with than he would have been with a couple of beers in him—though he was more cheerful.

Feeb was happy and full of energy and, for the first time in his football career, fearless. He began to do a real job on Conroy, which Conroy wouldn't believe, having played against Feeb the year before. It hurt Conroy's feelings, coming up so suddenly and in the middle of the game. "Goddamn, Siddoney," he said. "What's got into you?"

"Watch your ass, motherfucker," said Feeb. Then he giggled.

For three series of downs, Feeb pushed Conroy ten yards out of the hole on every play. Faro finally noticed what was happening, and he pulled Conroy out and put the first-string tackle back in. Then Feeb did the same job on him. And, finally, with Boniface on the Oglethorpe twenty-six, Feeb threw the first rolling block of his life, wrapping up the tackle's leg and breaking it.

"Goddamn," said Feeb. "This is fun. We're going to beat the motherfuckers."

Aaron gave Dimmy the ball two out of three plays, and on the ones when he wasn't carrying it, Aaron would fake it to him so he thought he was. The way he was hitting the line, Oglethorpe had to pay attention to him. And with Dimmy sucking in the whole secondary, Aaron flipped the ball to Whistler and sent him around end. The second time he did that, Whistler went twenty-six yards for the touchdown. At the end of the third quarter, the score was 28-13. The energy that Dimmy and Feeb and Whistler were generating spread out to the rest of the team, and though Faro substituted players till it looked like Oglethorpe was running a relay race from the bench, there was no combination that seemed to work. The Big Blue uniforms got dirtier and dirtier. But they couldn't stop Boniface. In the fourth quarter, Whistler scored on runs of thirty-five, forty-eight, and sixty-three yards. Dimmy got 114 yards through the middle, even though they were giving him the ball only two out of three plays.

After the fourth quarter started, Aaron kept begging them to let him throw a long one. "Drop a bomb," he said. "Last game. Drop a bomb." Jack kept putting him off, but after Whistler's third touchdown, there wasn't much reason to try to keep the game in their pocket any longer. The score was 49-13, and five of the Oglethorpe players were out of the game.

"Okay, Aaron," said Jack. "Drop your bomb."

Aaron faded back twenty-five yards—which was pure throwback behavior since not a single Oglethorpe player got across the line of scrimmage to come after him—then he cocked his arm and lobbed a sixty-five-yard floater out to Flasher on the five. Flasher waved to the Oglethorpe secondary, yelled "yoo-hoo" at them, then, when three of them came after him, spent the next minute and a half running around and dodging them between the fifteen-yard line and the goal before he stepped into the end zone to make it 55-13.

With one minute to go in the game, Whistler went around end, got into the clear, and ran all the way to the goal line. But he didn't go across it. Instead, he stopped on the one, put the ball on the ground, and stood with his foot on it waiting for the referee to come up.

"What're you doing?" said the referee.

"Blow your whistle," said Whistler. "That's where I want it."

The referee looked at him. "I don't think that's legal," he said. "Your knee ain't touched."

Whistler dropped down on his knee. "Blow your whistle."

"What the hell are you doing, Whitfield?" said Jack. "That's crazy."

"I'm tired of scoring touchdowns," said Whistler. "I'm a bored motherfucker."

Jack looked at him.

"Call time-out, Lynch," said Whistler.

"You going to draw straws?" said Jack.

"Call time-out." He motioned to Sullivan. "You go out," he said. "Tell them to send Demarco in."

"Demarco's hurt," said Jack.

"It's the last touchdown," said Whistler. He looked across the line at the Oglethorpe team. Four of them were sitting down on the field. Not kneeling—sitting. "Them cocksuckers're tired. Ain't nobody going to hurt him," he said. "Tell Coach we're going out the way we come in."

Sullivan started for the sidelines.

"You're going to play tackle, Dimmy," said Whistler. "Don't wait for nobody to give you the ball."

"Why would I be playing tackle?" said Dimmy.

"Because," said Whistler, "Lynch's going to play fullback."

Jack looked at him.

"Like you been saying, Lynch," he said, "we ain't never going to play football for Boniface no more. We're going to let you be a real hero for a change."

Lulu came limping up while he was talking. "What the fuck's going on?" he said.

So, with thirty-five seconds left in the game, Jack went over for the last touchdown, making the score 62-13. Then Whistler kicked for the sixty-third point.

Boniface got 563 yards from scrimmage — 384 of them in the second half. It put their rushing average for the season up over the Horse Rooney team of 1942.

When the score went up on the board, J. J. O'Brien took off his cartridge belt and swung it over his head, scattering silver dollars in a rain of shining cartwheels from the top of the flagpole he was sitting on at the time. "There's plenty more where that came from, boys," he yelled to the firemen who were following his movements at the bottom of the flagpole. "Plenty more where that came from." When he fell into the net, he landed on one of the coins and wound up with an imprint of Columbia on his right buttock.

As he walked off the field, Chicken Garfield was offered a job selling real estate. He asked the man to repeat the offer, then shook hands with him on it under the goalposts. "Do me a favor," he said.

"What?" said the man.

"Call me Chick."

Mary came up and put her arms around Jack's neck and kissed him right there on the fifty-yard line.

Just like the sportswriters said. It was the battle of the century.

# EPILOGUE

Some lives end in a way which is best explained as part of a divine plan. Not everyone likes this, but most of us come to it one time or another. The alternative is just too depressing.

Cowboy McGrath and Flasher O'Neil were killed near the Chosin Reservoir in Korea. That was on November 27th of 1950, four months after the Marine Reserve unit was called up out of Savannah. Flasher might have survived, but it was so cold the blood plasma froze in the packs, and they couldn't use them for transfusions.

Chippy Depeau drove his family car into the abutment of the Bull River bridge in the summer of 1949. It was a clear night, and he was doing more than ninety miles an hour at the time.

Some lives end in a way which seems consistent and fitting.

Bo Hoerner was shot and killed while rallying the men of his squad for a charge up Porkchop Hill. He was exposing himself more than was necessary but wanted to set a good example.

J. J. O'Brien was arguing with one of the officials over a call the official had made during the Bibb High game in the fall of 1952 when he suddenly stopped talking and a thoughtful expression came over his face. He keeled over rather slowly and gracefully and was pronounced dead of a heart attack twenty minutes later in the emergency room of Bibb Municipal Hospital.

And then there are times when lives work out quite well, and people do what they want and get what they want, and still are happy.

After high school Feeb Siddoney went to work in his father's produce store. He eventually became owner of a chain of curb markets. Every Sunday afternoon he takes his wife, Corinne, and their six children to Theodore's Ice Cream Parlor, where they all eat two chocolate fudge sundaes apiece. Sometimes Feeb eats three.

Ducker Hoy became a sergeant on the police force. For awhile he boxed semi-professionally, but after seven losses in a row he thought things over, then quit and got married. He is now a dutiful husband and father. He does what his wife tells him to do. She is a large woman and not particularly patient, but she has a lovely singing voice. When she sings "Danny Boy," Ducker cries.

Dimmy Camack inherited his father's shrimp boat. He lives out at Thunderbolt with his wife and four children. A fifth child is on the way. His wife is unusually attractive, and she cooks seafood wonderfully well. She is very protective of Dimmy because she feels he needs someone to look out for him. She is not a great deal more intelligent than Dimmy, but is smart enough to have figured out that much. Dimmy likes to pop the caps off bottles of beer with his thumb. His wife is very impressed by this and likes to watch him do it.

Frog Finnechairo went to work for the fire department. He has been decorated twice for bravery. Both times he rescued a child from a burning building by leaping out of a window with the child in his arms. *One* of the times he hit the safety net.

Whistler Whitfield went to Swainsboro State College on a football scholarship. He majored in a curriculum with the title "Technological Preparation." Since graduating, he has taken over the Miller Beer distributorship for the Savannah area and is doing quite well. He is not currently married but is keeping four women in different parts of town. He drives a red BMW.

LuLu Demarco won fifteen thousand dollars betting on college football games in the fall of 1949. This made a deep and favorable impression on Striper Wooten, who let him buy an interest in the pool hall. He and Striper are related in some distant and complicated way, but the chief thing is that they get along well. Lulu admires the way Striper smokes cigarettes, and Striper likes to hear Lulu hum.

Aaron became a gynecologist. He loves his work.

Jack went to Georgia Tech on a football scholarship. He didn't graduate because he missed Mary so much. Woe and general dejection forced him to drop out of school. He and Mary were married in the summer of 1949, and he got a job at the post office. Teamwork is important at the post office, and Jack likes the feeling this gives him. He has kept the vow he made to himself at Ballabee's Pavilion in the spring of 1946.

He and Mary are living happily ever after.

**THE END**